Seven Voices

VOLUME ONE

Seven Voices

VOLUME ONE

STORIES & REFLECTIONS

NORTH FORK WRITERS GROUP
LONG ISLAND, NEW YORK

The New Atlantian Library

THE NEW ATLANTIAN LIBRARY
is an imprint of
ABSOLUTELY AMAZING eBOOKS

Published by Whiz Bang LLC, 926 Truman Avenue, Key West, Florida 33040, USA.

This is a work of fiction. Names, characters, places, and incidents either are the product of the author's imagination or are used fictitiously, and any resemblance to actual persons, living or dead, businesses, companies, events, or locales is entirely coincidental. While the author has made every effort to provide accurate information at the time of publication, neither the publisher nor the author assumes any responsibility for errors, or for changes that occur after publication. Further, the publisher does not have any control over and does not assume any responsibility for author or third-party websites or their contents. How the ebook displays on a given reader is beyond the publisher's control.

ISBN-13: 978-0692505793 (New Atlantian Library, The)
ISBN-10: 0692505792

For information contact:
Publisher@AbsolutelyAmazingEbooks.com

OUR INTRODUCTION

Welcome to a different kind of anthology ...

We North Fork Writers Group members live on the eastern end of New York's Long Island, but our stories are not all about idyllic lives amid our area's famous beaches and vineyards.

Our tales span from ancient times to the 21st century in a range of topics and tones. Some are wry or funny, some are serious or sensitive, but all were chosen to reflect the extent of our seven distinctly individual "writers' voices."

While those differences add depth of contrast to the stories, their creative strength derives from our group's mutual support and encouragement. That personal bond has led to **Seven Voices**, Volume One, offering our first 25 stories for your reading pleasure.

Gene~Dave~Kit~Joyce~Jean~Susan~Teresa

OUR STORIES

NEW DAWN

DAVID PORTEOUS

Helen stirred; a languid stretching of legs and a stifled yawn. Her senses woke, quickly opening eyes to see if it had been a dream. Evidently not; Nick's clothes were where he had discarded them on the previously inaptly named love seat.

Bathroom? No, sounds like he's in the kitchen.

As her stretched arms liberated the yawn, she enjoyed recalling images from the night until she felt hair stuck to her lipstick's remnants. It got her hunting for a comb that hid in the bedside drawer's debris, and that got her thinking.

No, do it right. Brave it...face what I look like.

She crawled over the bed to a mirror, smiling at memories sparked by dislodged sheets until her reflection ended that. Helen stared at the mirror, too horrified to repair makeup; her eyes had locked on the image of her on hands and knees, body sagging like rolls of uncooked pastry dough. Nick knew her age, but had never seen her so vulnerably exposed; it was cruelly obvious in daylight that she was truly old enough to be his mother.

Hell! Looks like I'll find out if love is blind!

The quip eased her mood. She grabbed his T-shirt, pulled it on, and dragged the comb through tangled remains of yesterday's expensively salon-styled hair.

"Do I hear sounds of life? I'm fixing breakfast."

"Great!" she called back. "I worked up an appetite."

Hearing buoyancy in his chuckle pleased her as much as being its cause, so Helen found some makeup to put on as radiant a face as possible for him.

Nick mumbled: "Umm... There's something for you on the floor by my side of the bed."

All she saw was an eyeliner and an envelope, but when she added the pencil to her clutch of makeup, Helen noticed writing on the envelope. As it seemed to be song lyrics her squinting couldn't read, she took it and rolled back over the bed to get reading glasses from the jumbled bedside drawer.

A song? No...maybe a poem. And it's for me?

The idea of his writing a poem for her was so romantic that Helen was too amazed to focus on its meaning.

"Like it?"

Nick was at the door, trying to hide shy pride, but nothing else; he was gloriously naked to her. Unable to say that she hadn't really read it, she hoped a smile put him at ease as she said: "What I'd truly like is for you to read it to me so I hear your rhythm in it."

"So... You do like it?"

His eyes begged for praise, but she didn't know what to say and masked her silence by turning her smile sultry as she handed the poem to him. She saw his face flush with pride as he took the envelope, but he didn't even glance at it while reciting words that sounded heart-felt and he already knew by heart.

"Two people can always be
Two people;
Separated by their pasts,
And the lives they lead,
And the hand-worked masks
They often choose
To see themselves as being.
Two people can become one,

Sometimes.
They find a time when pasts
And lives and masks are blurred,
And then reach out, with care,
To touch and share
The precious joy of being:
Being loved."

He smiled. "I called it 'Two People', but it could be 'Last Night'...as it felt to me. Although, I think it suits any couple lucky enough to share what we had... Have."

No man had ever written a poem for her, nor exposed his emotions so uninhibitedly; she was speechless. Helen pulled Nick onto the bed and, as he propped on an elbow, admiring her, she peeled off his T-shirt. It was important to show him that she had learned to discard inhibitions during the night.

His gaze roved her body, an appreciative smile saying all she needed to hear as he told her: "Knowing you like what I wrote thrills me more than I can say!" Flushing with embarrassment, he smiled and added: "Well, no... Nothing could thrill me like you do. But I am glad you like it."

WISTERIA DREAMS ON THE NORTH FORK

TERESA TAYLOR

She called it Wisteria Cottage for years, her made-up name for it, though she never lived there. Twice a year, her parents spent a week at the cottage on Shell Point, once in the late Spring to unseal the house from its winter lockdown, again in the Fall to secure it against the coming winter and the raccoons. The idea of raccoons in the house charmed her. It was one more aspect of the place that made it paradise.

Julia was ten in 1950, the first time they pulled into the oyster shell driveway. She helped her father empty tools and work gloves from the '39 Pontiac's creaky trunk, but after checking with her mother, soon went off on her own.

She loved the silence, the loneliness, the empty narrow roads and stony beach just down the steps from the house. The air was pure salt. She filled a bag with scallop shells and golden orange jingle shells, which her mother insisted she wash in bleach before taking them into the house. She carried her pad and sketched the watery horizon and the occasional sailboat. She wrote diary secrets about the house contents, the dusty books, shelved arrowheads and locked trunks that filled the corners of the rooms. The wisteria vine hanging from an arbor over the side door fascinated her. The flowers grew upside down! She had never seen such a thing in her Brooklyn neighborhood, two hours away.

Back home, she told a friend about the magic place. "My father works with the owner," she boasted. "We can go there any time we want."

Her mother, who'd overheard the conversation, corrected her later at the dinner table. "Your father works *for* the owner," she said. "And we're lucky to be able to work there, even for a few days a year."

"When the owner dies, can we buy it?" She felt the intensity of yearning. It was something she'd never known. At night, she stayed awake for hours, creating scenarios, accidents and fairy godmothers to make the house hers.

In due time, the owner died, and the house passed to his grown children, who took upon themselves the seasonal tasks of opening and closing the house. Julia was 14, blessed with the oblivion of self-centeredness, but she never forgot the house. When she was old enough to have boyfriends with cars, she made every last one of them drive her the two hours east. She would point out Wisteria Cottage on the bluff above them as they walked the beach, shoes in hand, feet in the lacey foam of the shallows.

Years passed. Julia married unwisely, and was glad her mother died before the divorce. She lived abroad for several years, never feeling completely at home. Upon returning to New York, she found Bob, her true love. Her father, dying of cancer, asked Bob in a private moment "Are you going to take care of her?" After he died, they discovered that her father had left her a small but welcome nest egg.

She and Bob were married less than a year, both living and teaching in Brooklyn, when she started studying the *NY Times* real estate ads. The words 'Shell Point' jumped off the page into her heart.

"Babe," he said, checking the asking price. "There's no way we can swing that. I'd have to get two more jobs." He watched the light fade from her face. "Well," he said, "I guess I could add more hours of Drivers' Ed. And sign up for soccer coach this summer."

In 1979, they found a handyman special, with a two-car garage, a basement dedicated to alphabetically arranged tools, and a dusty attic. Best of all, it was on the same road as Wisteria Cottage, but on the opposite side, not waterfront.

Lee Thornton, the 77-year-old owner, had been living there alone for some time, since his wife had died. Now, he told them, he was going home to Kingston to live with his mother! A reminder, he warned, that kids "always come back." He appreciated their laughter and together the three of them reached an agreement. His demand was that he wouldn't have to clean anything out. "Just want to leave with my dog and some canned goods. The rest is your headache." It was a headache they could handle. They scraped the bottom of every barrel they had, and the nest egg took care of the rest, or at least the down payment.

Driving east every weekend, she looked for the landmarks that had thrilled her as a child. Most of them were gone, like the old windmill, but her sense of anticipation lived still. Julia felt the wings of angels each time she opened the shabby kitchen door into the house.

Whatever the weather, she walked daily to the end of the Point, inhaling the tart scent of juniper berries and butterfly weed. She never failed to walk the right-of-way next to Wisteria Cottage, checking to see if the owners were in residence. She hoped so, wishing the old house the comfort of human presence. The wisteria reached ever closer to the roof, a cascade of blooms or, in the fall, seed pods that Julia liberated and planted behind the stone wall that bordered the road in front of their house.

By the early 80s, Julia and Bob had each found a job on the North Fork. The weekend trips, now in reverse, declined to the point that they sold the Brooklyn apartment. Julia woke up every morning grateful and unbelieving. This is where I'll live and die, she thought, stretching pleasurably in Lee Thornton's bed.

They made few changes to the house. It was a rambling farmhouse, dating back to 1920. Their research showed it to be one of the first houses built on Shell Point. Respectful, they restored rather than renovated, in spite of the quirky layout. One of the four small bedrooms had two doors, both leading for no apparent reason to the same corner of the long angled hall. All three bathrooms featured white subway tiles, decades old, and mosaic floors of tiny black and white hexagons, no bigger than nickels.

They noticed the subway style came into vogue several times over the years, each time to be replaced by a new trend. They left it the way they found it. One bathroom had a tub just big enough for a small adult to sit in. A soaking tub, someone called it. Julia did not expect it ever to hit the trend list. In any case, they did not change it.

Julia and Bob started to know their neighbors. They met the old-timers at cocktail parties, at communal barbeques on the causeway leading to the mainland, and on rights-of-way leading to the beach. Bob did some weekend carpentry for waterfront residents, building beach stairs and adding decks. The two began to feel settled-in. The older residents enjoyed their youthful energy and there was no shortage of dinner invitations to be reciprocated.

Shell Point had always been wealthy, a summer hideaway for moneyed residents of Garden City, Manhasset and Manhattan. As time passed, it remained wealthy but was soon no longer hidden. Lots were cleared, stripped of trees, new houses built, some of them impressively huge, some impressively ugly. There was negative reaction from some of the longtime residents. Julia felt some discomfort, but in her continuing state of gratitude tried to live by a determination not to "pull the ladder up" just because she had discovered heaven.

She and Bob considered themselves fortunate newcomers, not entitled to feel special. In an effort to bring "ordinary people" out east, they decided to open a low-key bed-&-breakfast. Just two rooms with adjoining baths. To break the ice and soothe the unease of their more established neighbors, they first opened their home gratis to those who had family members traveling from afar to attend weddings or funerals. It earned them trust and approval. When the B&B actually opened to the public in the mid-90s, there was little resistance.

And people came! Weekends were booked from early June to late October. Julia left a guestbook on the coffee table that filled quickly with appreciative comments from guests as far away as the Faroe Islands, which they learned were off the coast of Scotland. Bob did the breakfasts, playing short-order cook as he constructed piles of French toast, pancakes or omelets. They spent quiet evening hours discussing the oddities and charms of their guests when the house was theirs once again.

Their goal to share their happiness was soon met, perhaps beyond their intentions. One couple who arrived at the height of the dot-com bubble to "check out the vineyards" meant exactly that. They were there to buy one, and they did. Several guests hooked up with real estate agents and eventually bought homes on the North Fork.

Bob and Julia began to feel the pain of success. The North Fork was being discovered, for which they shared the burden of guilt. The development of Shell Point continued. There was astonishment and some dismay when a buyer razed an older home on the bay side and built a 9,000 square foot French villa. This was followed by a string of similar practices. It became the custom to destroy the house one bought and replace it with something grander. As the old guard left for Peconic Landing or the Elysian Fields, newcomers added paved driveways bordered with Belgian block, and stone pillars topped with wrought iron-caged lamps. There were few oyster shell driveways to be found. For that matter, there weren't many familiar faces to be found either. There was a troubling day when, chatting with an Hispanic gentleman who was mowing the lawn next door, Julia realized she knew landscapers who worked the many properties better than she knew the people who lived there.

At the end of a particularly busy tourist season, on one of her daily walks, she headed as usual toward Wisteria Cottage. In the driveway was a contractor's truck. On the fence was stapled a sheet of green paper. On closer look, she recognized it as a building permit. A second floor and a first floor extension were to be added, the extension on the south side. It dawned on her slowly. It was the side with the wisteria arbor over the door.

Of course. Julia was not surprised, only a little sad. She started to walk down the right-of-way, only to be blocked by a sign that read "Private - No Trespassing." Undaunted, she struggled her way through the off-path vegetation to the beach.

She tried to focus on the bay, on the sky. Once on the beach, she realized there was less of it than she remembered, even at high tide, a result of the storms and the consequent erosion, most visible alongside the docks and groins that had been constructed over the past few years. Julia sighed and climbed a section of the bluff that brought her back to the road.

Continuing her walk, she stopped to pull seeds from the dried butterfly weed at roadside. Someday I'll plant them, she thought, stuffing them in her pocket. We'll have a small garden. There will be sidewalks and houses with shell driveways and people who go to work every morning and people sitting on porches with awnings and the school bus will come and there will be children and dogs, all of whose names I will know.

AUNT MIMI'S WORLD

JOYCE deCORDOVA

Peculiar, eccentric, or, as my mother would often say, "not one hundred percent" describes my Aunt Mimi - and the following stories are slices of her life. If someone you know reminds you of Aunt Mimi, you have my congratulations - and my condolences.

AUNT MIMI AND THE U.S. NAVY ...

Let's face it. Aunt Mimi was a flirt. Wait, I take that back. Actually, she was a combination of a flirt and a patriot. I really didn't know that until I came across a commendation she received from the U.S. Navy for doing her part in the war effort during World War Two. After reading the citation, however, I've concluded that as far as the flirting part goes, she may have gone beyond the call of duty.

I grew up during the war and I lived in a tenement on Manhattan's Upper West Side with my grandmother, my mother and Aunt Mimi. The entire family of mother, father and five children (Aunt Mimi was the fourth) had emigrated from Italy during the early 1900's and, from the time they were twelve, the children worked in factories in the Garment Center. Catching on quickly, a fast learner, Aunt Mimi rose in the ranks as a pattern maker for an upscale fashion house called Hattie Carnegie. Not only was it a well paying job, but she also could buy their up-to-the-minute stylish clothes for less than wholesale prices. She had a small figure and the samples fit her beautifully. She was a pretty woman with hazel eyes that had an impish look to them as if she was scouting for her next adventure. Throughout her lifetime, she did her share of scouting and the U.S. Navy was one of her adventures.

During the war, aside from "Uncle Sam Wants You", other posters were plastered all over, urging everyone to get involved in the war effort, either by contributing time, money or ... Aunt Mimi took this seriously.

Most Friday and Saturday nights there would be a different officer (it was always an officer) who would climb our five flights of stairs, and in full uniform and with cap in hand, knock on our door and ask for Aunt Mimi. I was never allowed to answer the door lest her date might think she had a child (she didn't) ... A child just wouldn't go with Aunt Mimi's image. She presented herself as a fun-loving, carefree girl (she was in her late 30's at the time) doing her part for the war effort by brightening the lives of our servicemen. God bless her!

So off they went ... Aunt Mimi intent on showing the officer the time of his life. She would tell me that he was being shipped out that week for Europe and he might never return home, so it was incumbent on her to do all she could to make the evening memorable. I went to bed and slept soundly...and sometimes dreamt of Aunt Mimi dancing, drinking and laughing the night away with that probably doomed officer who always had a smile on his face. Come to think of it, I never heard Aunt Mimi come home. (Or did she?)

After she died at the age of 88, I went through her things. Here is a note of caution for all of us: If you don't want something to be found after you die, destroy it by the age of 70 because, after that, life is basically about dodging a bullet and you wouldn't, unlike Aunt Mimi, want to be caught with your pants down.

The commendation was from U.S.S. Flying Fish (SS-229). At first I thought that it must be some sort of joke and that there was no such ship in the Navy called The Flying Fish. There was. It was a submarine that was very active during the war, yet suffered only three casualties. On March 9, 1943, three crewmen from the *Flying Fish* died of drinking wood alcohol at the Royal Hawaiian Hotel during R&R in Honolulu, Hawaii. These three seamen would be the only casualties that the crew of the *Flying Fish* would suffer during the War. When I read this, I thought of a party boat cruising the Pacific.

The commendation states "for outstanding service as Entreneuse on the wardroom table of a U.S. submarine during Wolf patrol". At first I thought the word "Entreneuse" was an exotic use of the word "entertainer". I looked up the definition of Entreneuse and I have concluded that it is a misspelling of the words "entre nous", meaning "off the record' or "between us". That sounds more like it, especially when it was awarded for her "ability, intrepidity, and gallantry in furnishing accurate movements in a Hula performance to the Sheik of Araby".

The commendation goes on to say that her conduct raised the morale of the officers present. I wonder if morale was the only thing Aunt Mimi raised. Just like Rosie the Riveter symbolized women doing their part in the war, so did my Aunt Mimi.

AUNT MIMI AND THANKSGIVING...

All of the family worked ten to twelve hour days and after work they would go home to their ghettos. It was comfortable. They understood the food, the customs, the language. They could relax. They belonged. Yet, the children were also part of the "New" world, where English was spoken and the music was hot and the skirts were short and hair was bobbed. They were constantly learning and absorbing and trying to fit in to both places. For many immigrants, it was a tug of war between this new America and Italy. But, as far as Aunt Mimi was concerned, Italy was losing.

From the time she set foot on US soil, she was determined to be part of this new world of hers. First she changed her name. Domenica became Minnie (as in mouse), a name given to her when she arrived on Ellis Island. She then changed it to Mimi because it sounded more sophisticated and, well...upper class. She refused to speak Italian except to my grandmother, and she read the society columns of the Journal American to keep up with the latest gossip and scandals. She would browse through exclusive boutiques and copy patterns of the most stylish and "in" clothes and sew them herself. She didn't consider herself Italo-American. No hyphenated identity for her. She was an American!

A holiday, unique to America, was Thanksgiving and Aunt Mimi was going to celebrate it in true American style. I was about 8 years old at the time and I remember Aunt Mimi decided to make a turkey with yams and pumpkin pie and cranberry sauce and all the trimmings for a real American holiday. This left the rest of the family totally confused. As far as they were concerned, they gave thanks every day for having a roof over their head and food on the table. For them, this Thanksgiving holiday was a day off from work. They could sleep late, listen to the radio, make a bowl of pasta and relax. And what was this big fuss about a stone called Plymouth Rock where Pilgrims, those people in crazy clothes, landed on this rock almost two hundred years ago? We Italians had rugs that were older! If these crazy Americans wanted to cook all day making a special meal about a Rock, let them.

Other American holidays were also confusing to the family. Labor Day was a day that you *didn't* labor. Memorial Day was meant to be a day of reflection and to honor those who had died in Wars. But then, why was there music, parades and celebrations?

But, as far as Aunt Mimi was concerned, the family just didn't understand and their attitude wasn't what being American was all about. It was about embracing the traditions of a country that you will probably live in for the rest of your life. You needed to belong.

So, on Thanksgiving morning, she woke up at 5am, made a stuffing from a Joy of Cooking recipe book, stuffed the turkey and put it in the oven for about 8 hours. Then she made the rest of the fixings and scattered autumn leaves on the table as decoration, giving it what she considered an "autumn feel". My grandmother was horrified ... dead leaves on the table where you eat!

Because she had worked so hard, we all sat at the table and dutifully ate foods that had a strange taste to them. The pumpkin pie tasted like starch. The turkey was huge and took forever to cut, made awkward by Aunt Mimi's insisting that my uncle carve it at the table a la Norman Rockwell. But there was a limit. After fifteen minutes of our salivating, my uncle grabbed the legs and pulled them off.

Aside from the homemade wine, Aunt Mimi served Cider. "The only kind of fruit that I drink is wine", said my grandmother. "Apples are good for your teeth and your digestion, but that's it!"

I must admit that the more wine we drank, the better the food tasted. And so the tradition of celebrating Thanksgiving a la Italia began, except that the next year there was also a tray of lasagna that my grandmother made to go along with the turkey.

Although Aunt Mimi had her moments and was considered by the rest of the family as a bit off, she was the one in my life who expanded my world. I didn't just belong on Manhattan's 96th Street; all of Manhattan was open to me. In fact, all of the United States belonged to me! I was an American, just like Aunt Mimi and pumpkin pie...and Thanksgiving

AUNT MIMI AND RICHARD NIXON...

While I was growing up in the late 40's in Manhattan, the world was in pretty good shape. Korea hadn't happened yet, so there was a welcome hiatus between wars. My mother, grandmother, Aunt Mimi and I still lived in a fifth floor tenement on the upper west side. There was a Cushman's Bakery on the corner, a shoe repair shop, a butcher, and a general store owned by Mr. Spry. At night, I could see the neon sign across the Hudson River in New Jersey with the word "Spry". I thought it was our grocer, Mr. Spry, and I was impressed that he was so famous and had his name up in lights. I didn't know Spry was also a brand name for lard. People were friendly, but not intrusive. They looked out for each other in a New York kind of way. It was "count on me if you need anything, but otherwise, leave me alone." In short, it was a neighborhood with normal people doing normal things. But not if you had Aunt Mimi in your life.

My mother was two years younger than Aunt Mimi, and probably because they were close in age and because it was family and my mother was a nurturer, my mother bore the burden of Aunt Mimi throughout her life. As my mom got older, that burden fell on me, an only child. They both married and became pregnant at about the same time. Mom had me, Aunt Mimi had a still born. They both got divorced and went to live with my widowed grandmother. And there we were, four women; three generations living in a tenement on the upper west side.

Living with Aunt Mimi wasn't easy, but it wasn't all that bad either. She loved me and I loved her sense of living in the moment and always looking to have a good time. During her long periods of normalcy, she would take me on day trips all over Manhattan ... The Circle Line, the Statue of Liberty, somersaulting down the hills of Central Park, the Zoo, The Empire State Building, ice skating in Rockefeller Center and even the Stork Club! But sometimes it was hard for me to enjoy the good times because I was always waiting for the other shoe to drop.

"Sensitive" was a word used by my mother to describe her. (You must remember that my mother was kind.) When Aunt Mimi lived with us, she insisted that the bathroom door stay open when I was in there so she could keep an eye on me because she didn't want someone to drown me in the tub. I was seventeen at the time.

When she would come home from work, I always looked into her eyes, and if I saw a vacuous stare, I knew something was brewing. Her job? People staring at her on the train? Food tasting funny from the deli? I would hug her and talk about my day and desperately try to distract her from her fears by sharing some of my own. Speaking of fears, she was one of mine. I feared and loved her at the same time. She never laid a hand on me, but I never knew that she wouldn't. There was always the threat of...what? A beating? Her grabbing me and hurling me out a window? Some children have a sense of resiliency. I was one of those. I could survive her craziness and calm her down no matter what. Then I would be safe at least until the next time.

She held down a good job at Hattie Carnegie, an upscale fashion and costume jewelry house in the 40's and 50's. She was a pattern maker and made good money. At 55, after grandmother died, she decided it was time to learn to drive; she did, and took a job traveling across the country, selling jewelry at department stores from New York to California. Quite an accomplishment for a 55-year-old woman in those days. But then she was found running naked in the streets of

Los Angeles, wide eyed and fearing anyone around her. My uncles had to fly out there and fly her home.

I married in my early 20's, had five children in 8 years and went to live in Brooklyn in the early 60's. Mom and Aunt Mimi lived in the Bronx. You would think that I'd be worried about them because they were getting older and living far from me. After all, I was an only child. But the distance felt good. Even though I had five small children and my home at times was unbelievably chaotic, I felt normal. Although I missed Aunt Mimi's joie de vivre, I didn't have to deal with her episodes and paranoia or my anxiety that she could snap at any moment. I didn't have to deal with her fears that were palpable and running through me as well as through her.

Then they moved to an apartment four blocks away. Aunt Mimi retired; mom didn't and that is when she started going downhill. The shoe did drop...again

"Joyce, you need to come over. It's about Aunt Mimi"

My heart flip-flops to the floor. "What happened? Is she okay?" I asked.

My mom's voice dropped to a whisper. "She's talking to President Nixon about the war in Vietnam."

"Is she on the phone?"

"No, she has the blinds drawn in her room and she says Nixon is on the blinds...just like a TV screen except that he is speaking only to her."

I dropped everything, asked a friend to watch my children and went over there.

Aunt Mimi's eyes were wide with a mixture of anxiety and excitement. "Too bad you came now Joyce, they just finished their conference and left".

"Who?" I asked, trying to appear calm and casual.

"Richard Nixon and Henry Kissinger. It was about Vietnam".

I succeeded in putting a look on my face that I believed having Nixon and Kissinger discussing the War in Vietnam on your window blinds was perfectly normal. We chatted, and then she said she was tired and took a nap.

I told my mother that Aunt Mimi needed to see a psychiatrist. My mother was anxious, remembering the days when Aunt Mimi had to be hospitalized and medicated. I tried to assure her that we would be catching this episode at the beginning and all would be well. I so wanted to believe that.

I made an appointment with a psychiatrist for the following week. My mother said she would come with us, but I knew she didn't want to go. She was frightened and, even though it was unspoken, she was resentful, fearful and imagining what it would be like to once again have her life filled with the paranoia, delusions and all that came with it.

Aunt Mimi agreed that it was a good idea to see a doctor. I didn't tell her he was a psychiatrist. She hadn't been sleeping well and she thought that maybe some medication, like a sleeping pill, would make her drowsy and less anxious. Whew! Step One = success.

We took a train to the city. Wrong move. She was agitated. Too many people. Why were they all looking at her? She held me close. I had to be careful. There were bad people out there!

The doctor was a distinguished, gray-haired, impeccably dressed and handsome man. Aunt Mimi's kind of guy. She had always been a flirt...but that is another story. He told me to wait while he and Aunt Mimi had a private conversation. I was more than happy to leave her with him. I was so tense ... *I* needed meds!

Twenty minutes later, he called me in. Aunt Mimi was smiling. He was smiling. He said he and Aunt Mimi agreed that some medication to "take the edge off" would be a good idea and he wrote a prescription for Haldol, which I knew was an anti-hallucinatory drug. We shook hands. Aunt Mimi asked if she could give him a kiss. "Of course," he said. She did, smiled, and we left.

I breathed a sigh of relief. Not bad. She's cooperating. Once the meds kick in, her life and ours will be okay. Step Two = success.

I hailed a cab. Even though I knew it was expensive to go to Brooklyn from the city, I couldn't bear another train ride with her. Her fears, the tension, the anxiety had been palpable. I needed to smooth out.

In the cab, the smile became a grimace; her mouth firmly set. She turned to me and said, "That doctor is an idiot. Does he really think he is fooling me? I know he is for the Vietnam War. He wants me to take drugs so he can manipulate me and I will be one less person against the war! I know his type. Smooth talker; bullshit walker," she mumbled angrily.

"But Aunt Mimi, you said you would take the meds. You know they will make you feel better. You'll get a good night's sleep"

"You don't understand," she said. "I *need* to feel tense. I *need* to be on the alert! Good thing I didn't tell him about this morning's meeting between Nixon and Kissinger!"

At that point, I decided to just go with the flow. I couldn't walk away from her. We were enclosed in a cab! "That must have been an interesting meeting Aunt Mimi. What did they say?"

She turned to me with a horrified look on her face. "Joyce, where are your manners? That would be eavesdropping, and I don't do that sort of thing."

We were on the Brooklyn Bridge. No, I didn't jump. After all,
she was my Aunt Mimi and she was family.

GOD IN APPLEWOOD

KIT STORJOHANN

Most people were uncomfortable around him because of that concave chest of his, a byproduct of having every known or experimental treatment for consumption tested on him. As I found out over the course of his stay at the asylum, most of his life he'd been hooked up to strange machinery, or been submerged in tanks of freezing or boiling water, or taking countless potentially toxic pills and pastilles. Every doctor with a theory about what might get his lungs functional had taken a pound of flesh in their vigorous pursuits, leaving him crooked as a spoon. He would joke, "They said they must have scooped out my heart."

To most he was an off-putting lunatic, but he found a friend of sorts in me. At the very least, I was a faithful chronicler, a means of conveying his story to the world. No one wanted to hear my war stories about brute survival in the endless mud. Those of a romantic sensibility want to hear stories of heroism, bold one-man charges that saved the world from the rampaging Huns. To those who study the broad sweeping game of history, my part is less noteworthy than that of a pawn on a chessboard.

Those who say they want to hear about only the horrors of war truly want to hear only that it was horrible and be spared the details. I had stories of friends shitting themselves to death as we hid like moles in the trenches. Spiders and maggots invaded every mess kit and supply box and were eventually as indistinguishable from our rations as poppy seeds. I didn't hold some comrade dying in my arms, nobly swearing fealty to his sweetheart at home after valiantly holding off an enemy charge. No, I had stories of teenage boys crying futile tears which rolled down scorched cheeks from liquefied eyes. Anyone taking too long to light his cigarette would drop in a heap, hit by a bullet from across the blood-strewn No-Man's land.

I coughed and starved and prayed my way through seemingly never-ending rotations through the trenches. Once it was over, all anyone at home wanted to talk about was hanging the Kaiser and how much money everyone in America stood to make from our victory, and that war was over forever. I kept the cough, and tried to forget everything else.

The next year was made of coughing and macabre parades of caskets of people I didn't know lurching down the streets. My cough got no worse, though, and I drifted along, picking up work wherever I could. A friend mentioned that an asylum upstate was paying good money for orderlies, because from time to time lunatics had to be restrained, need to be shown order. He said that former soldiers found it a natural fit, and meager pay was offset by room and board.

A stone wart on the horizon resolved into a veritable temple as I approached. Set apart from nearby towns, it was intended to be something akin to a dumping ground a generation ago. I was hired after a short interview with a couple of tired-looking doctors. "You'll suit," said one.

I did. The work was more tranquil than I'd thought, mostly cleaning and getting the inmates to line up so they could be marched to the mess hall or the showers or the dormitory.

As new discoveries in medicine led to new treatments, shackles were abandoned, their bases pulled from walls and the chains sold as scrap. Hydrotherapy was much touted then, and rooms were given over to tubs and hoses. Corridors were lit by bulbs high off the floor and tiny barred widows that lurked up near the ceiling. My first time up a ladder to replace a bulb, I realized I was probably higher off the floor than I'd ever been before.

There wasn't much time off, but I spent my time in my little room, reading from stacks of books I'd collected from wherever I could find them. Homer was followed by a tawdry romance set during the Civil War, then on to a history of the French monarchy, and I relished the alchemy of words in any spare hours I could find. Routine suited me just fine, and I was grateful to have found my place.

I didn't know that I'd still be there through several permutations of the asylum, or that I'd be gradually promoted to supervisory levels. There was no way for me to see that those dark corridors would now be bright and colorful with windows all through the building, or that screaming would all but stop, and I'd never have thought patients would check themselves in, and thank us profusely as they checked themselves out. I couldn't have imagined sitting in an office, signing requisition forms for supplies for the orderlies of today; that I would be the one interviewing them, or that I would be looking for new recruits to show compassion rather than raw strength.

I was too young then to foresee that my cough would grow to fit in perfectly with other men my age, but I knew that I coughed every time I looked at the dented-chest inmate I had befriended back in those early years. Even at its worst, my cough never compared with his. Whenever he coughed, his hands would fly to his mouth as though trying to keep his guts from jumping out to escape his exertions. The sound started as a low wheeze desperately clawing in enough air for the ordeal to come, then sputtered its way out in rattling paroxysms that shook his whole body and left him trembling as though from a chill for minutes afterwards. Doctors assured us that his condition had been treated to the point where he could no longer infect anyone else, but it seemed to me that they tended to keep their distance from him.

Parchment-hued skin seeped out from his collar and sleeves as timidly as if it had never seen the sun before, and he was rarely able to force a smile from that gaunt, sallow face. And yet, listening to him talk you'd think he was smiling all the time. A smirk always slipped into his tone, even as his face stayed drawn and taxed.

After his last stint at the sanitarium, he coughed his way through shift work at a steel plant until they let him go. He'd slyly attributed his relatively comfortable time after that - staying put at a boarding house and still having three squares a day - as a result of being in with some of the better known figures in organized crime. He mentioned to me a few times that he was doing "odd jobs for Dutch." The truth, as I found in dribs and drabs, was that what he did was scrounge, and he was accomplished at that artistry. Loose change found its way into his hands. He could pull a surprising amount of usable meat off a bone or flesh off an apple out of the trash, and he thrived on thin stews of garbage. At a time when staying alive through that Depression was an accomplishment, he did it without letting anyone know he was ever less than flush.

I never found out exactly what landed him in the asylum, but he'd often wink and tell me confidentially "I know too much." I just knew that the other orderlies called him a run-of-the-mill loony deluded about being close with famous people. Doctors tossed around numerous terms, with dementia praecox being the most-often overheard.

"I ain't crazy," he said. "I just know a lot. For instance, I could tell a pretty tale about Garbo. I knew how her voice sounded before you did. Believe you me, that gal has a set of lungs when she gets going. Hoo-wee. Say, got a snipe?"

Why he always asked for a cigarette when it was sure to send him into a fit of coughing was not something I ever got to understand. Nor did I figure out what impelled him to talk and laugh only to me. Around every other inmate, every other orderly and nurse, he was taciturn as a tombstone. Doctors' questions prompted only perfunctory responses.

"Yes, Doctor. I'm still coughing."

"No, Doctor. I'm not awake after lights out anymore."

"Yes, Doctor. I'm drinking the milk like you said to."

Later he would confide to me that he stared at the ceiling all night long, while rows of men around him snored in peace, taking refuge in dreams that carried them outside the asylum, or wallowed in nightmares they couldn't forget.

"I see their dreams sometimes," he said. "It's not right seeing into another man's head, though. And I hate milk. Damn stuff never sits right with me. City juice'd suit me just fine."

He'd greet me as I came on shift each morning, giving me a salute and a smirk, and then cough into his hands for a minute or so. If no one was watching, he'd check them for blood.

A doctor whose name I've never known came to the asylum for a few months, bringing several bags and boxes. We orderlies hadn't been told that he was coming, or why, but once he opened his mouth he was Fritz to us. That was his name when we talked about him amongst ourselves, but of course we always had to address doctors as Doctor, so names were incidental as far as we were concerned.

Fritz insisted on meeting each inmate individually, and needed an orderly at his command at every single meeting. As had become customary whenever something new came up, I was assigned to the task. I helped Fritz set up a room with a big table and unpacked his bags, all filled with paper, crayons, clay, or finger-paints. One by one, I led the inmates into the room for Fritz to interview. He worked his way through a repertoire of questions about who they were and where they had grown up.

I was meant to be as incidental as furniture during these meetings, but I listened to the life stories of these men I'd known only as one in a line of inmates, or from strapping them to a cot or locking them into a tub. I wish I could say I found some common thread running between all of their stories - one thing that had gotten broken and made them different from me, or from Fritz, or from anyone walking around on the streets - but I never did. Fritz, on the other hand, encouraged them to keep talking and nodded as though he understood their struggles completely. Then he would ask them to draw a picture of themselves. Most would, and they'd scratch out with something generic with no more thought than a child would offer: two eyes, a nose, a mouth, and ears where they belonged. A few came up with asymmetric horrors of screaming skeletal heads or human-monster hybrids. Fritz noted all of this, and followed up by asking them to sculpt their childhood pets from clay, or to paint their happiest memory.

In the following decades, Fritz's approach moved from being bizarre to accepted, then standard. Decades later I'd be sitting at a desk in my own office, signing off on a parade of therapists with hundreds of new ideas about cures. Inmates became patients. No longer locked in freezing baths, they now had electricity shot through them, writhing and convulsing before somehow discovering some tranquility that had previously eluded them. Visionaries no longer strove to have the inmates sterilized in order to build a better world. Something akin to mercy works its way through the system, and that leaves me hopeful as my career nears its end.

Sometimes I think it's a pity my hollow-chested friend didn't get to see it, but it's doubtful if he could have drawn breath much longer. He was younger than I, but while my cough has resolved into something intermittent and grumbling, his was always a mark of imminent demise. After watching the war and the flu and the times carry his family away, he was left with the imaginary comfort of his well-known connections. In time, they all faded into stories he was too tired to tell, even to me. He just got to be tired of being sick, tired of being crazy, tired of being alive.

When interviewed by Fritz, he avoided offering any information while answering questions. Everything got a curt answer, and it was clear he had no wish to elucidate.

"How many siblings do you have?"

"None."

"You're an only child, then. Ja?"

"I had two sisters and three brothers."

"Had?"

"They died."

"I see. Are your parents alive then?"

"No."

He didn't add to that, so they just sat in silence for a long time until Fritz slid a sheet of paper and a handful of crayons across the table. "Would you be willing to draw me a picture?"

"I never learned how to draw."

"Well, we're not looking for art. I'd just like to see you draw a picture of yourself. Ja?"

"No, thank you sir."

"Well, perhaps you'd prefer to draw another member of your family. A sister or brother, perhaps."

"No. Thank you, sir."

Fritz set a gelatinous gray blob on the table. I'd seen it pulled and shoved into dozens of shapes already by the other men. Most were crude, but Fritz had studied each one as though it were an x-ray, and taken copious notes before he wadded it back into amorphousness. "Perhaps you'd like to sculpt something then. Ja?"

"No. Thank you. Sir."

In the silence that followed, Fritz looked like he was staring at a particularly difficult mathematic equation. My friend started to shake, and then he coughed and wheezed for several minutes while Fritz looked on. His hands finally fell onto the table, but he knew enough not to check them for blood flecks in the sputum in Fritz's presence, and acted instead as though he had a cold. "Say," he said. "Do you think I could get a snipe? I'm out as usual."

Some of us orderlies ran the inmates through calisthenics every few days, and Fritz heartily approved of it. Our regular doctors saw it as a vaguely good idea, but never showed much enthusiasm, probably because they hadn't thought of it. To some of the old sawbones, it was revolutionary not to have the inmates shackled to the walls, and few of them had any fervor for revolution. Fortunately, more progressive minds allowed our charges some measure of humanity, and it was in the courtyard that my friend first saw the face of God.

On one day after summer's warmth had faded we enjoyed a respite from several weeks of rain. Inmates shivered as they jumped and ran in place on a soggy quilt of leaves in air that was sharp, free of mist. Ravens stabbed the light, darting between skeletal treetops, making bold declarations that echoed through the grounds. Tufts of orange and yellow clung to branches here and there, but most had already surrendered. We lost a handful of trees in the storm and they'd lain like corpses for a few days amid the fallen leaves.

As his pallor indicated, he had little patience for anything that took him outdoors, but I took it upon myself to get him out on that first dry day. He made a token effort at the calisthenics, then leaned against a wall, breathing deeper than I'd ever seen before. However, it wasn't the exercise that had caused it. He was transfixed on the face of God, a divine discovery he'd made in the asylum yard. Of course, I had no idea he was in a spiritual reverie until I walked over to him and asked if he was okay.

"Yeah," he said. "I just realized I was looking at God."

"God?"

"Yeah." He pointed at a fallen apple trunk. "I need that."

"I don't think that's a good idea. Why do you want it?"

"I gotta get God out of it. He wants to be let out of the wood."

"Stay here," I said.

Knowing that no one in his right mind would let one of the inmates start carving up a tree, I looked for Fritz to mention the idea to him. I found him sitting in an empty dormitory room, making notes about the empty bunks as though each man had left traces of his dreams on his pillow. After I'd explained the situation, he gazed at the ceiling for a while, mentally debating every facet of the possibilities. Yet he was clearly having difficulty in hiding his enthusiasm, and when he finally met my gaze and agreed, I was only surprised at the restraint he showed in his simple "Ja."

Regulations for the procedure were written up, and for once I didn't mind being assigned to an unusual duty. In fact, I was more than happy to volunteer some spare hours of my own time to supervise my friend's progress. Before starting work, he was obliged to strip to his skivvies, and to leave his clothes piled outside the room. I would then follow him inside and lock the door behind us. "If he tries anything', I was told, "you're on your own."

The tools were lain out in a line akin to a surgeon's table, and he was only permitted to take one at a time, then return it to its proper spot before being allowed to pick up another. Not that this bothered him at all. He was slow and methodical, and although the progress seemed remarkable to me, his hand never rushed. It simply slid along the surface of the wood as though seeking some invisible opening, then it would rest for a long time letting each superfluous splinter fade away in his mind's eye until the line was perfect. Then he'd raise his chisel and begin to shear the wood in slow, deliberate strokes.

When I asked him if he'd had a lot of woodworking experience, he answered as incredulously as if I'd asked him if he'd spent a lot of time on the moon. "Never," he said, and began feeling for the next section to be carved.

For a guy who got wheezy from walking around the yard, he had a surprising amount of energy. He never complained about the implements he was given, no matter how old and dull they'd become. His hand would simply find its place on the wood and linger for a long time. Then he'd pick up a half-rusted chisel and start to gently peel away everything that was not the face of God he'd seen hiding in the cadaver of an apple tree. I had little doubt that he would have stood there and carved the entirety of his vision in one session if I'd let him.

He never coughed while he worked. I watched him for hours at a time, and never saw him raise his hand as a shield or heard the low warning wheeze. Whenever I told him that he would have to have to stop his carving soon, he would ask for a cigarette and continue working with it dangling from his lips until it was nothing more than a nub. Then he'd stub it out, and replace whatever tool he was using at the time.

I'd take everything from him before I unlocked the door and led him back to the dormitory or the day room. He didn't complain when time was up, but I could see his mind going back to the unfinished lines of the figure as he sat with the other inmates. In every waking moment he longed to return to the emerging sculpture; I obliged him as often as humanly possible.

As he laid his hand on the figure one day, he announced, "This will be the last day. I'm finished after this."

"Good for you," I said. "You'll show it to Fritz then?"

"I don't see why."

"Listen," I said. "He wants to help you. He's an odd duck, even for a Jerry, but he means well enough."

"I know."

"So you'll show him, then?"

"Yeah." I handed him a cigarette, and he raised his chisel to the trunk of the figure, to give it his own signature of sorts.

When Fritz inspected the figure that day, he could not fail to recognize the bowl-shape of the statue's chest. "This is you, ja?"

"Yeah. It's a statue of me."

I could see no resemblance between my friend and his creation. After he'd finished divesting the trunk of everything which wasn't God, the end result wasn't even lifelike, but more akin to a hint of a person than the intricate marble statues of Greek ruins. I hadn't followed art trends, so I had no idea that such half-formed figures and less-than-realistic reflections of the world were accepted as profound statements. The divine creature was taller than a man; even I had to look upward at its blank mask face. Smooth curves of eyes crept out to stoically regard the world, their tearless gaze sorrowful rather than judgmental. An aquiline nose and peaked brow were the only other concessions to human facial features. Its frame was gaunt, as though some ancient spirit comprised of little more than flesh strung over bone had been transmogrified into wood. It leaned and stepped forward slightly, both hands at its sides, as though resignedly walking the earth.

After circling the figure several times, Fritz delightedly shook my friend's hand and then mine. Interest spilled into euphoria, and Fritz began to praise all three of us, himself most emphatically.

Numerous interviews were scheduled in following days and my friend's entire demeanor changed. He coughed more discretely, and walked with the same pride as the orderlies and the doctors. He made no strange proclamations to me, nor dropped any names. I was present at an interview with Fritz where he spoke as though a fog had been lifted. Things were clearer, he said. He was no longer angry that his family had been taken from him, that his chest was caved in, or that he'd be coughing and hacking forever due to something he couldn't have helped.

Months of being an entirely new man on the ward, an ostensibly cured former lunatic, ended in my friend being given his release. He shook every doctor's hand and wished all of the inmates well, even though he'd never socialized with them.

I walked him out the front gates and along to the bus stop at the end of the road. "Gotta snipe?" he asked.

I handed him a cigarette. "So, do you know where you'll go now?" I asked.

"Nah. I just couldn't be in there anymore. Hearing other guys' dreams, knowing that Greta's missing me. Boy won't she be surprised. Look after God for me, okay?"

If I had an orderly under my supervision who behaved as I did, I'd definitely have dismissed him, and probably had charges pressed if at all possible. Whatever reason I had for not speaking up to anyone in charge is still a mystery. The only explanation I have today is the one I had then: it simply wasn't my story. A clearly demented man hoodwinked everyone else and walked out the door, leaving nothing but a wooden God that everyone but me believes is a self-portrait. My role was nothing more than a means to whatever end he had.

Reports of how he died varied, and none had the strength of anything more than rumor. Some said he'd simply coughed more and more until there was no room left for breath. Other reports said that he headed out west on the rails and had frozen to death in a hobo jungle somewhere. I also heard that he was beaten to death in a dope den over some imagined slight, but whatever the story was, he didn't even last three years after being released. By then, Fritz was long gone, triumphant in his success and presumably spreading his wisdom to other asylums.

Time has re-forged this place many times over. I am too old to keep up with new ideas and must leave it in the hands of younger people. In light of my impending retirement, I was offered the sculpture which has stood in the alcove of the hallway near my office since I'd played midwife to its birth decades ago. It is not mine, I've decided. I have joked to my colleagues that my wife would kill me if I brought more junk into the house. The truth is that I have merely passed under the sad eyes of this God and cannot claim any ownership of it. However, I ordered a plaque which I have affixed to the base where it stands:

"GOD IN APPLEWOOD. ANONYMOUS. 1932"

I'll let posterity wonder why God appears to be missing a heart.

I'M FROM NEW JERSEY

GENE RACKOVITCH

My wife Harriet was about to leave the store where she rents space from Lydia of Lydia's Antiques in Greenport as the last two customers approached them. One was a local man, known to them, the other a handsome young stranger in his mid thirties. He dressed well, but not exceptionally; in fact the striped shirt he wore hung loosely out of his black trousers. The shirt had a look of the forties. Though well groomed, there seemed to be a look of confusion about him.

Harriet and Lydia were talking to the local customer as the stranger stopped at the door, turned around and said to no one in particular, "Where am I?"

Lydia and Harriet looked at each other and Lydia said, "Why, you're in Lydia's Antiques."

"No, no, I have to ask you a question."

Lydia looked at Harriet with a knowing smile and said, "Oh my, this sounds serious."

Harriet replied, "I'm sure it is," and the three locals stood there with broad smiles on their faces.

"I'm from New Jersey... Is this the Hamptons?"

The seriousness of the man's expression dispelled doubt that he was joking. Still, Harriet, Lydia and the local customer looked at each other quizzically. It had to be a joke.

"No," said Lydia, "you're in Greenport."

Without loosing the lost expression he said, "Oh."

Harriet added, "This is the North fork of Long Island. The Hamptons are in the South Fork."

"Jeez, I thought I was in the Hamptons. What is the North fork? I really wanted to go to the Hamptons."

The local customer, though ready to leave, decided to stay and see what the outcome would be with this Jerseyite. He usually wasn't one to add his two cents to conversations, but felt he had to say something to put the man at ease.

"Why do you want to go to the Hamptons? We have lots of interesting things to see on the North fork. Greenport has a lot of Historical buildings, a park with a Carousel, and the Marina is full at this time of the year. We have wineries, and a great many farm stands on the North fork, and our restaurants are fine... Seafood is fresh from local fishermen. Or just walk around and check out our galleries. We've got some fancy artists here."

The Jerseyite said, "Well, I still want to go to the Hamptons. I'd like to see the luxury. Ya know...the million dollar houses and the rest of the luxury there. I want to see the beaches, and all that stuff. I like luxury!"

"But," Harriet intoned, "even if you go there you won't see the houses. They're hidden by hedges a million years old, and I expect if you decide to go in they'd probably send the dogs out after you." She turned to Lydia and smiled.

"Yeah," the Jerseyite said. "But I like luxury. How do I get there?"

"Well," Lydia said, "you can take the ferry out of Greenport, and get the other ferry out of Shelter Island... That will take you to Sag Harbor."

"I wanna go to the Hamptons."

"Well, you'll be on the South Fork, and that will lead you to the Hamptons."

"Does it cost any money, the ferry?"

A quick "Yes, it can be expensive," came from Harriet.

"Nah, I don't want to pay. I just want to get there. Is there any other way?"

"You can go back to Riverhead and swing back to the south fork from there," Harriet let him know.

"But I want to go to the Hamptons."

By now, a little frustration was settling on the locals.

"Well, it's kinda late now," said the local customer. "Even if you go, you'll probably have no place to stay. It's real crowded over there. Even here in Greenport at this time of year there is no place to stay."

"Nah, I ain't gonna stay here! Ah Jeez, I really wanted to see the luxury. I like luxury." Carrying his frustration out the door, he left.

Lydia turned to Harriet with her arms raised in the air. "We get 'em all, don't we?" she said, and bid Harriet a good night.

DICK AND JANE

Jean Schweibish

The house was quiet as Dick stepped into its cool, gloomy interior. Tossing his keys onto the front hall table, he bent to set down his briefcase. Straightening up, he paused at the sight of his face in the mirror above the table. He saw the tension in his jaw and the slight tilt to his head, and thought *she's not here, relax*. Instead, without shifting his gaze from his own eyes, he stood motionless, listening. He scanned for telltale signs of his wife's creeping insanity, its tendrils always seeking to wrap around and overcome him. He heard nothing but the abrasive call of a blue-jay outside and, more distantly, the constant shushing noise that was the flow of traffic on the nearby highway. His mind drifted.

For more years than Dick cared to think about, he had approached the front door of this house, their house, with an anticipatory dread. Reaching to put his key in the door, he would immediately experience an unbearable tightness in his chest, fear would constrict his breathing, and adrenaline would begin coursing through his body, making his heart race. How many times had he come home to find a stranger had taken over the familiar face, form and voice of his wife, Jane? He had no idea who this person was, making demands he could not meet or accusing him of things he could not have done. Over the years, feeling off-balance at first, then numbed by Jane's outbursts, Dick only reacted, never actively thinking about the fires of madness she willfully set in their lives.

Family had to be put off, and friends had eventually stopped calling. Little Nell had to be kept out of her mother's way – *out of harm's way*, as Dick thought to himself. From day to day, hour to hour and eventually minute to minute, Dick had no way to predict which Jane might be staring out of those dark, haunting eyes, and what might next issue from those lovely, but lost to him, lips.

For months, Dick had hunted through scores of Internet sites when he should've been working on billable hours at his firm. He tried every key word he could think of in his search for answers to his wife's aberrant behavior. He read about schizophrenia, multiple personality disorders, manic depression, and at one point, only half in jest, demonic possession. He found no answers.

Jane did not see any change in herself. She perceived a shift in their household but firmly placed any difference on Dick. He was the one demanding things from her, expecting too much from her, not supporting her, not pulling his weight at home, out drinking with his office friends. She would begin one of her verbal onslaughts by calmly and coldly telling him that he was a failure, working a job where he'd never advance and never be paid a living wage, delivering an oft-repeated mantra "We'd be living on the street if not for my trust fund money!"

Motionless in front of the hall mirror, no longer seeing anything in it and lost in the past, Dick rewound to the beginning of Jane's bitter accusations, all of which had tiny components of truth in them, just enough to have made Dick doubt himself. Take the trust fund comment. They'd been living in a rental apartment for their first couple of years of marriage, and they agreed it was time to look to buy their own place. Jane's money *had* paid for the house Dick was now standing in, but it was at Jane's insistence. The bulk of the trust fund account would pay for all but the closing costs, she'd said. The house, a two-story cottage on three-quarters of an acre, had several smaller outbuildings on the property, including one ideally suited for Jane to set up her sculpting studio. Dick had protested that they should take out a mortgage to buy the property, and not touch her money, but Jane had made up her mind and could not be dissuaded. She told him that this was her contribution to their life together. He would be the partner who went out into the working world, she the partner who quit her day job to pursue her dream of devoting herself, full time, to her art. This was the property that could make life just about perfect.

That had been eight years ago, and Jane had worked hard, making a name for herself with her small sculptures of the human form. It was not such a well-paying reputation that Dick could give up his day job to pursue his own dream of becoming a professional photographer, but, still, he didn't actively hate his job at the small law firm he worked in as an associate attorney. He enjoyed his clients, his salary was good, and he had free time to work on photography skills on weekends and vacations, and he'd been slowly renovating one of the other outbuildings on their property to make a small studio and darkroom. Jane had been right – it seemed their life was just about perfect.

When Little Nell was conceived, four years into their marriage, Dick and Jane were surprised at first, and then pleased at the thought of becoming parents. They'd been too self-absorbed to consider children, and had never even discussed whether kids would be part of their future together. Dick had looked forward to a new subject for his camera and took photos of Jane as Madonna as she grew larger with their child. Over the next nine months they talked about what life would be like when "baby made three." Jane made sketches of fetuses, babies and toddlers, thinking ahead too about a new, evolving series of sculptures she looked forward to creating.

Neither of them had any clue how much time would be carved out of their lives to accommodate Little Nell after her arrival. Nor were they aware of the coincidental and stealthy arrival of an opportunistic parasite, with the alliterative moniker of "post-partum psychosis" which was delivered into their home alongside the baby delivered into their arms. Jane would be irrevocably altered by its affects, and though it took time, Dick would learn that the woman who had been his wife had packed her mental bags and left for a territory of irrationality that there would be no return from. For a long time she masked her disappearance with a cunning ability that allowed the old Jane to appear as needed, like some holographic image of her former self appearing in the landscape that had been their marriage.

In the first couple of years of her life, Little Nell was looked after by Jane, while Dick was at the law office. Jane first thought she could continue her sculpting, keeping Nell nearby in a bassinet. But Nell was a fussy baby, demanding a great deal of attention, sleeping in fits and starts and never completely through any night. Jane began to lose weight and have trouble catching up with sleep, and then she stopped working in her studio. She was constantly concerned that there was something seriously wrong with Nell, often calling Dick at work in panic, sometimes at the most inopportune times. He'd either be forced to tell her he'd have to call her back, or explain to his client that there was a family emergency call and excuse himself from a conference. For 15 months, following Nell's delivery, Jane continued to exhibit un-Jane-like symptoms of depression. Early on, her doctor had said this was not unusual, labeling the symptoms part of "post-partum depression." Symptoms ran a wide range from overwhelming sadness, to an inability to deal with anyone but Dick, to anger at Dick, and to fear of handling Little Nell. There were long periods of time when nothing Dick said or did could shake Jane out of whatever altered state of mind she functioned from. Long-time inside jokes between the two of them, which had never failed to make her smile, became arrows she felt he intentionally and maliciously aimed at her. His clumsy and unpracticed attempts at helping with household chores and the baby created irritation and sharp outbursts from an impatient Jane. Sex became a mere memory, Little Nell its sole reminder; even attempts at brief hugs or a quick peck on Jane's cheek met with cold indifference. These symptoms were all acceptable in the eyes of the medical community – after all, they had that very common and specific label to attach to Jane's behavior.

Dick finally suggested hiring a nanny. They could surely afford one now. Jane would then have time to herself, to get back the color in her face, gain some weight, catch up on her sleep, and maybe even start creating again. Jane acquiesced, but nanny after nanny came and went, each dismissed by Jane, who became convinced that they were mistreating Little Nell, or stealing from them, or taking drugs, or spying on Jane when she napped or tried to work in her studio.

By month 18, Jane was not getting over her so-called post-partum depression and her doctor was "getting concerned." Dick was past the stage of concern and into full-blown hopelessness. Vitamins, rest and patience had done nothing to reverse or improve his wife's state of mind. Jane, for her part, had found a haven in avoidance – of Dick and of Little Nell, as best she could, since she was the child's main caregiver. She had gone back into her studio when the last of the nannies had been fired, and begun sketching ideas for sculptures, but her sketchpad was filled with horribly disfigured humans, some with spikes protruding from their skin, others with torn-open torsos and creatures escaping from inside like newly hatched Boschian spiders. Faces etched with pain had eyes raised and mouths open in silent screams. Dick, coming home one evening from work to see the light on in the studio, went to see how Jane's return to work was progressing. She made no attempt to hide her drawings, nor did she encourage his review of them. Dick, disquieted by these dark renderings, asked his wife where the inspiration for these new pieces-to-be was coming from. Jane's distracted reply was an airy "I don't know, they appear in my head when I close my eyes, and when I've completed putting one down on paper, another pops up, then another, and another." Dick, scanning the studio, noted the quantity of sketches strewn about the space; Jane was indeed cranking out these little horrors one after another as if on some perverse and invisible assembly line.

Jane had made perhaps a half-dozen maquettes from the sketches to show the owner of the gallery that represented her, but he would not take these pieces. They were too disturbing, he said; their presence made his staff uncomfortable, and, he imagined, such things would only drive his customers out of the gallery. But, as he'd represented Jane since the beginning of her career, and he wanted her to have success with her new work, he would show the new pieces to a gallery owner known for carrying edgier works and having a clientele that relished the unusual. The new gallery, *The Other Side*, was more than pleased to have an artist of Jane's reputation creating work suitable for their market. The small models were put on display, marked "Not-for-Sale." Those buyers interested in what the maquettes promised were encouraged to leave a substantial, and non-refundable, deposit for the piece or pieces of their choice. Within a few weeks, all of the sculptures were spoken for.

Sometime around Little Nell's second birthday, Dick realized his Jane was never going to return, and he did his best to take care of Nell and stay out of this doppelganger Jane's way, especially avoiding her studio. One day a call came in for Jane from her new gallery, and Dick reluctantly walked the phone out to her. True to the new Jane, she was abrupt with him, took the phone roughly from his hand, and turned her back on him to carry on her conversation with the owner of *The Other Side*.

This was the first time in almost six months that Dick had stepped inside the studio. As he looked around at what appeared to be a series of sketches for new work, bile rose up in his throat. Pinned to a large wall-mounted corkboard was a familiar, childish face – Little Nell's – but Nell deconstructed, each of the sketches more disturbing then the next. There was something truly repulsive in a mother depicting her child in these dark and ugly ways. As Dick carefully swallowed, a great wave of fear washed over him and he felt terribly cold. He turned and numbly made his way back to the house to make a call on his cell phone.

What followed was a series of therapy interventions, starting with a visit to the OB/GYN. Ultimately, a psychiatrist was consulted and Jane was prescribed an experimental drug that turned out to be the final push over the edge for her. By the time Little Nell was two and a half, it was obvious that Jane could no longer live without supervision, nor outside of a controlled environment.

Dick felt the emptiness of his marital vows weigh heavily on his heart the day he signed Jane's commitment papers, and drove her to the State Mental Hospital. She was still on the experimental drug and was lethargic and easily maneuvered. She made no protest, nor did she make eye contact with Dick at any point, until they stood at the main desk of the hospital, an orderly at her side, hand carefully gripping her elbow. Dick tried to kiss her cheek, murmuring he would come to visit regularly and that she would be well looked after here. It was only then that Jane finally looked at him and slowly and carefully said "You don't get rid of me so easily, you pathetic bastard." Then she turned away, looked up at the orderly and began a slow shuffle down the hall without once looking back. Dick clenched his teeth, biting back his impulse to call "Wait! I've changed my mind!" This was his wife, for Christ's sake – how could he allow her to be put away in this place? Then he thought about Little Nell, and the words were never spoken aloud. Once Jane had been diagnosed and confined in the State Hospital for the Mentally Disabled, Nell, now four, was enrolled in nursery school for the hours Dick was at work.

Dick continued to stand frozen in the vaguely musty hall of the house until his mind's directive translated to his body, his hands slowly uncurled, his breathing became slower and deeper, and he rolled his neck to one side until he heard a gentle pop. He moved down the hall towards the kitchen, anticipating the cold drink he would grab from the refrigerator before heading upstairs for a quick shower, donning his after work jeans and polo shirt before heading out to pick up Little Nell from nursery school. Poor kid, she was usually the last to be picked up by her parent, but not today. Dick had finished up work early enough to make it home before going for Nell, and on this rare occasion would even be one of the first parents to arrive at the nursery school. He smiled, thinking ahead to her surprise and pleasure at waving goodbye to the other kids for a change.

Pushing the swinging door into the kitchen, Dick stopped at the sight of the open back door. He could now hear quite clearly the blue jay and its mate calling back and forth in the maple trees in the back yard, as he tried to recall if he'd been distracted enough to have left the kitchen that morning without closing the back door. When he couldn't conjure up the details of that particular morning's rush to get cereal into Nell, and down the cup of coffee that was his own breakfast, before they hurried off to the day ahead, he idly wondered what the jays' exchange was about.

Cold drink forgotten for the moment, Dick walked slowly to the back door, still trying to pick up the pieces of the puzzle of that morning's particular routine, and with a notion to peer out the back door and try to catch sight of one or both of the still noisy jays. Looking into the backyard, his eyes fell on something boxy and pink lying on the walkway to his wife's art studio. It was Little Nell's "Hello Kitty" backpack, the one they'd packed up together this morning, and the reason they always ran late – Nell's indecision about what she needed to take for the day, Dick's patience in never rushing his daughter. The spontaneous explanation that sprang into Dick's consciousness was that somehow Nell had left the pack absentmindedly as she searched for some object she'd left in the backyard that she'd wanted to take along to nursery school. But surely he would have noticed?

Like a sleepwalker, Dick steadily and quietly pushed out through the kitchen door to the backyard, no further thoughts of that morning on his mind. He walked up to and stared down at his daughter's Hello Kitty backpack as if the little cat character would offer up an explanation. Then he heard the low sound of two voices, the high-pitched giggles of Little Nell, and a softer, adult voice that sounded a lot like Jane. He looked up from the silent Kitty towards his wife's studio, pulse quickening, and cautiously made his way down the walkway. Reaching the studio, Dick carefully pulled the screen door open and saw Jane in her element, crafting a sculpture from brown clay, while talking to her creation. Her "creation" was Nell, already half-encased in the clay, still giggling as her mother wrapped her small torso in it.

Dick's eyes travelled from this scene to the kiln in the back corner of the room, its indicator light glowing red. "Jane! What the hell are you doing?" Dick said. "Stop it! Now! I mean it Jane!" Nell had stopped giggling at the sound of her father's angry tone, and wide-eyed, looked from Dick to Jane and back again, now unsure about the game she and her mother had been engaged in – Nell as human armature.

"Hello Dick, it's so good to see you." Jane softly replied. Stepping away from Nell, she smiled warmly, and started towards where he stood inside the door. "I'm here on a brief visit. I had some unfinished work to complete and they said it would be good therapy for me to spend some time in my studio." Caught off guard by Jane's reasonable tone of voice and his confusion at her being there, Dick let his wife approach him. She had gotten close enough to reach out to him, a familiar gesture that promised a gentle caress along the side of his face. He was unaware of the syringe in her other hand until she'd plunged it into his neck. As he felt the room darkening, and he began to crumple before her, he could just make out Jane's last words to him. "You're just in time, I'm almost done with Little Nell ... and then it's your turn, Dick."

SURVIVAL

DAVID PORTEOUS

Eddy Kelly scowled into an underground corridor of businesses, muttering: "Ah, these poor bastards get their lives stolen workin' in this tomb with no winders!"

He pitied the staff he saw behind glass doors and the poor bastards in doors still ahead, one of which he saw was less well lit. On instinct, he hurried by all the pretty receptionists to that door and its bamboo blinds muting the light inside.

"Found ya! All righty... Let's go in an get started!"

The room's arrayed equipment told Eddy that anyone who came here had to keep it neat. He then saw a bamboo screen and a desk's end behind it, the only place anyone could be, so he went to it. A gray-haired, wiry Asian man sat cross-legged in the desk chair, but his wearing only Rugby shorts was what took Eddy's attention.

"Name?"

Eddy's gaze flew back up to the man's face. "Whatsat? Oh ... It's Eddy ... Kelly, sir. This your place?"

As the man nodded, he asked: "Edward?"

"Sure, that's all of it. But I'm called Eddy, sir."

"Not sir. I am Sensei."

"Senz-eye?"

"Hai."

"Hi? What? Are we startin' all over again?"

"Hai is yes. I use many Japanese words here."

"So...you've not got a real name? Just Sensei?"

"In here you call me Sensei." His eyes glinted. "But I have a name. Tetsuo Fukinamisa."

"Titso Fookin-a-miser? Yeah, Sensei's lots better'n that."

"How old?"

"Me? Sixteen last July, sir ... er, Sensei." Eddy waved at the desk's visitors' chairs. "Want me to sit?"

"If walking along that hallway tired you, hai. If not, no."

Eddy tried to lighten Sensei's terse manner with: "Wanna keep me on me toes, do ya?"

"Why sit? You want to enroll for Karate, yes?"

"Sure, but... Like, I thought I may as well sit. You are."

"Two lessons, free. Do what I say, not what I do. And do not disobey or question me in this dojo."

"Do-jo? Jap for gym or some such? Got it, an seein' it's all pretty clear now, where do I sign?"

"First I must see clearly that I can accept you."

"I've got the money."

"Not everyone suits Karate. Do you drink beer, smoke, or waste your mind on video games?"

Eddy replied as curtly: "No, no, and not much."

Sensei grunted. "Do you wrestle or box?"

"Box? Did. Still could, if I wanted. See, I used to box at a CYO on Saturd'ys ... Catholic Youth club."

Sensei's eyes narrowed. "You look to have the body to be a boxer, so why not now?"

"Ah, it's just that I...ah... No, it's a long story."

"I am not busy. Tell it to me."

"No, really?"

"Lesson two was do not question what I say. Tell me."

Eddy let out a sigh of fatalistic disquiet; parts of the story would expose a life he didn't want to explain. Perhaps his conflict showed, because Sensei nodded at a chair and Eddy heard a softer tone say: "Sit, relax and tell me your long story, Edward. Breathe deeply, be comfortable."

"But ... Well, it's not so easy as ya might think to talk of. It's not just the boxin', ya see ... It's ... um ..."

"So start by telling me why you started boxing."

"Usual reasons ... Life's tough. Ye've gotta learn to defend yerself. I mean ... know how to win a fight, an all that."

"Did you learn how to win a fight?"

"Oh yeah. Never lost in twelve bouts. Just amateur club stuff. Still...twelve for twelve's not bad, eh?"

"Better than not bad, Edward. But it does not tell me why you became a boxer."

Eddy explained that his family expected it. He told Sensei of Grandpa Padraig Kelly, a top Irish Lightweight in the 1970s, and his Pa, Michael 'Mad Mick' Kelly, Welterweight Champ of Britain's Royal Navy whose career was cut short by cut-prone eyes. From even before the family left Ireland when Eddy was seven, Mick had tried to train his son to chase the boxing glory that had eluded him.

Sensei asked: "So you learned to box for ten years?"

"More like learned to take a punch. Pa taught me when he could, an' he was a champ in a Navy full o' hard men. Hit me all over in sparrin'. He surely knows how to hit...an hurt."

Sensei's eyes again narrowed. "You trained ten years for only twelve fights, so when was your first?"

"I was fourteen."

"Your Pa did not want you to start younger?"

"Fucken did! So'd Grandpa! Both nagged me, an Pa took me to the club soon as I was ten ... That's when the boxin' program will take ya."

"You were not accepted, or chose to not fight?"

"I wouldn't! I knew what I didn't wanna do."

Apparently intrigued, Sensei asked: "How did your Pa treat you from then until you did box?"

Eddy's face showed unease, but he said wryly: "After he'd beat the shit outta me back at home? Ah, he was lovely. Hollered ev'ry fucken day 'bout how I'd let down Grandpa, an' didn't bother to be sober to spar with me. Yeah ... that Pa o' mine's a real prince."

"So tell me about your fights, and why you stopped."

As if to balance saying too much already, Eddy described those years unemotionally, but he saw them in his mind like a dark video with a harsh ending ...

Eddy got home from the CYO feeling some pride, but hating the long bus rides to the club and back. He had no option in that, or in learning to box; the CYO's boss, Father Ryan, knew of Mad Mick's sparring sessions. But Eddy spent most Saturdays only training, because no boys of his age had grown to match his size.

He tried to reach his room before his parents saw his cut-up face, but as he passed the TV room his father peered through cigarette smoke to say: "Got a bout, boy? Sixth, was it? Win?"

"It was my eleventh. An yeah, I won again."

Mick shook his head. "Yer a feckin myst'ry. I know ya can't box fer shite. Ya always look like shite after fights... Yet ya say ya win. How can that be so?"

"I told ya! No one hurts me. An' Father Ryan stops any fight if a boy's hurt. Why keep askin'?"

"Coz ya always look like ya feckin lost! Ya must pound the real losers to pulp."

"I broke poor Tony Benco's nose today."

"Poor Tony nuthin', ya feckin' pansy! Ya won's what matters. Now, get me another beer!"

While in the kitchen, Eddy pondered a hint of pride on his father's face after hearing of Tony's nose. It sparked an idea that became: "Ya know, I got Tony with that right uppercut ya taught me... Held it back to explode up as I stepped in. Wish ya'd seen it."

After considering that, Mick nodded. "Me too. I might take ya next week ... to give ya tips 'tween rounds, like."

Eddy stifled a grin. "Father Ryan says I'll be fightin' a new Italian boy in his Parish. I might need tips if he's tough."

"No feckin' Dago's tough as us, boy! But sure, I'll take ya, an' I'll buy ya a burger if ya win. But it's ice ya need now. Get some on that face."

Eddy's grin looked like thanks to Mick, but it was joy from winning that round: his father would drive him to the CYO in their old VW Beetle and spare Eddy from the tedious bus rides.

It didn't go smoothly; Mick slept-in, hung-over, but unable to face breakfast so they got to the club in time to avert the ire of Father Ryan. The Priest introduced them to eighteen year-old Vito Bruno with apologies for just seeing that Vito was too mature and experienced for Eddy.

Mick growled: "Not for a boy from my fam'ly when his old man's watchin'! He'll fight."

Eddy ignored Vito's more-man-than-boy advantage as he donned boxing gear, hoping the Priest kept Mick away from him between rounds. His father sat ringside as Eddy and a volunteer trainer, Police Officer Riggs, got in the ring. Now hoping that Mick wouldn't call out during the fight, Eddy began to mentally prepare for the three two-minute rounds.

Two rounds went as he expected, and as Riggs wiped blood from him between them, Eddy saw Mick fidgeting in his seat. After round two, Father Ryan came to see Eddy's damaged face and ask if he could continue in the last round.

"Oh, sure! Ya know blood don't bother me none, Father, an Vito can't hit hard... I let him try all he wanted."

When the amused Priest backed away, Eddy looked at his father's seat; Mick had left it and the room. He started the final round worrying that his father had not waited to drive him home, but taking punches got his mind on what had to be done.

Eddy showered and dressed, still afraid the VW would not be there, but he found his father leaning against it, smoking and frowning. Eddy approached him warily.

"C'm'ere, eejit! So *that's* how ya fight? Let big shites keep hittin' ya till they're feckin' cocky an drop their guard... So ya drop *them* an' the ref stops the bout. That's it, right?"

"Somethin' like that, Pa. Yeah."

"Then hear me. One day you'll face a boy big as that one an' just as fast with his feckin' hands ... but one that hits as hard as you. I'll tell ya this right now ... He's goin' to feckin' kill ya!"

Eddy nodded; they rode home in silence ...

"See, Sensei ... Pa was bein' nice. Best thing he ever did for me was give a real boxer's advice that I can never be one. Sure, he's a shit, but he let me see I had to give up boxin' afore I got too beat up."

"I see such advice could be from care, Edward, but if it was him at his nicest, do you hate him for everything else?"

"Hate Pa? Jasus no! Ya askin' cos I said he's a shit? That's got nothin to do with it. Ya can't hate family!"

"I ask because you won fights wearing padded gloves, but when you can break stacks of wood or cement blocks with Karate, breaking a man's bones will be easy."

Eddy snapped: "What? Think I'd learn Karate to beat up Pa? I said I don't hate him, so don't you say such bullshit! Us Kellys are a boxin' fam'ly ... We have rules for fightin'!"

Sensei let a smile flicker. "I am glad. But you cannot learn here if I have a doubt about why you came."

"Then I'll find some other fucken do-jo! I said I won't use it on Pa ... If ya don't believe me... Fuck ya!"

Sensei responded: "I teach a Martial Art, Edward. It was a weapon of war ... now it seems to be merely for fitness. But Master Senseis in Okinawa taught me to teach Karate as more than just a Black Belt to brag about. Understand?"

"No. I don't need a war weapon, so ... Wait! Yer owner *an'* teacher? Got no young fellers teachin'? But yer older'n Pa!"

"Old means having experience in using skills. I teach skills to all who can gain from learning. I think that, maybe, I can teach you, and you will learn more than Karate skills."

"Only maybe? Whaddafug've I gotta do so ya know?"

"Tell me why you refused to box at ten, but let a Priest get you to do it at fourteen. Was it what your mother wanted?"

Mention of his mother made Eddy want to leave the prying Jap, but he now wanted to know why he'd learn more than Karate there and decided to risk opening up those tough-to-explain topics.

"I'll tell ya this much ... I started boxing 'cause o' Ma. She's why I looked up this place on the Internet, too."

Eddy took a deep breath to relax before recounting...

His parents always argued when Mick came home smelling of beer; that was always. Mary would rebuke Mick for wasting money, and for how his faults ruined their marriage; he'd blame her family's interference. Eddy's refusal to box at age ten only increased Mick's frustration, but by then he knew that one beer landed him in just as much trouble with Mary as a dozen, so he chose the latter.

Before he was ten, Eddy saw his Grandpa and Pa as boxing heroes, but after that birthday Mick's sparring became so brutal Eddy thought that his mother might also fall victim to his father's violence. He was surprised to find that she didn't share that fear.

"Sure, yer Pa's got faults, but he'll not hit me. His Pa hit yer grandma, and it marked him. Yer good to care, but I'll be fine. It's yerself I fret for if he lashes out at you."

For two years, Mick vented his ire while sparring, but that changed when Eddy grew to be his father's size by age fourteen. If Mick stormed away from Mary's yelling and found Eddy in range, he'd slam a vicious punch into his son's shoulder ...

"After years o' takin' Pa's whacks, I was glad to get someone else's defense lessons. Best I knew from Pa was keep clear o' him, but I had to stay close by when he an Ma rowed to look after her. That's when Ma told our Parish Priest that Pa's sparrin' beat me up, an he got Father Ryan to push me inta the club's boxin'."

Sensei understood, but asked: "If you let opponents hit you, what defense did you learn there?"

"That Copper Riggs kept me practicin' ... blockin' rights with me left as I threw a right. Other trainers knew I hit hard, so had their boys keep me off with straight lefts, an' try rights only if they saw openings. So I gave 'em openings, but just blocked rights till the end, an they didn't expect the thump that dropped 'em."

Sensei allowed a grin. "Good tactic, Edward! Ignore pains and then unleash power. It was your form of Karate focus, and it makes me surer of what I can do for you. But two things puzzle me. You gave up boxing on your Pa's advice... Did you two still spar?"

"Sparrin' stopped soon after. What's puzzle two?"

"Why replace boxing with Karate?"

Before replying, Eddy scanned the dojo. "Nice. Clean, tidy. Feels good here. A safe feelin', ya know?" He saw Sensei wanted a better answer, but asked: "Want more truth?"

"Please. My instincts tell me there is something about your father in why you want to learn Karate."

"Yer right. Follow yer instincts, do ya? I do, an now they're tellin' me to talk about stuff I never do ... Tell ya the whole ugly ... The fucken shameful truth."

Eddy described what resulted from the Saturday that his father saw him fight at the CYO club ...

It took Mick until Friday to accept that his son would never be a world champ. He arrived home drunkenly belligerent and the row that night with Mary got nasty faster than usual; he pounded walls as if it demolished her rebukes. Eddy heard Mick's anger growing and rushed to the kitchen to be ready to shield his mother.

His red-faced parents stood toe-to-toe, hurling insults like grenades, but Eddy ignored their yelling and focused on his father. When something his mother said provoked Mick to clench his fists, Eddy leaped in front of Mary, deaf to her plea to stay back because of the danger to him.

"Back off, Pa! Ya'll not go usin' fists on Ma!"

"Shut the feck up! What'll ya do? Hit me?"

"I don't wanna, Pa, but I will 'less ya back off."

"Feckin eejit! I'd drop ya afore ya closed a fist!"

"Maybe, but yer drunk, Pa, so don't try it!"

Eddy saw a right hook coming and instinctively blocked it with his left arm as he put all his power into a right uppercut. Mick crashed onto the floor, groaning. Mary looked from her son to her vanquished husband, and then ran from the room in tears ...

Eddy recounted that episode watching Sensei's expression evolve from interest through anticipation to culminate in a smile and the exclamation: "Excellent, Edward! He never hit you again ... right?"

"Right ... an' he's the one stopped sparrin'. Ma's calmer. Her an' his yellin' now just lets off steam. Him and I hardly ever talk to each other, but I don't care about that, or what he thinks."

"And Karate? Where does that fit in, Edward?"

"I know it's disciplined. I want that so I can hold off from thumpin' Pa if he pisses Ma off. See, I want him to know I can bust bricks, so I could bust him bad ... But only I'll know I'd never do it."

Sensei finally uncrossed his legs and stood up. "Then you should also know that I am now pleased to enroll you, Edward."

"Can't ya call me Eddy? It's sort o' me name."

"A boy's name is not fitting for any young man who I will be teaching all that I can."

OUT WITH THE OLD

KIT STORJOHANN

Voices of distant crows dwindled from a dusky shriek to a croaking warble in the ears of the servants, then dissolved into silence. A face, reduced by a niqab to eyes swollen with a deeper sadness than most people manage to express with their entire countenance, was just on the inside of the glass, watching the last light of the year thin out and fade to darkness. The owner of the eyes turned back to her fellow servants, Arabs in worn robes drifting around the perimeter of the great room of the inn. For a moment they had surrendered their constant duties of scrubbing and sweeping to watch the sun go down. An old man leaned crookbacked on his broom, and practically wept as he resigned himself once again to some private grief. The guests of the inn, two British officers and a young woman, did not notice him. He sighed, silently met the gaze of every other Arab - who gave him wordless assurance in the form of a very slight bow of the head - and went back to sweeping.

One officer sat in the most comfortable chair in the place, a red leather wingback affair. With dark hair and a sharp mustache, he was habitually batting down a sly smile every few seconds when it threatened to appear, replacing it with a practiced scowl. The other officer had light curly hair and was pacing about with an endless excitement as though every few steps held some marvelous possibility he had not managed to uncover the last dozen times he'd trodden them.

The woman was cheerfully dressed in tailored khaki, as though prepared to accompany them on some glamorous safari. Perched cross-legged on a stool, worrying the scarf around her neck with her tiny fingers, she kept looking at the door.

The great room of the inn was remarkably clean. Although the innkeeper was by no stretch of the imagination a harsh man, cleanliness was something on which he was utterly unwilling to compromise. An Arabian Jew with long memories and deep roots, he seemed to have some kinship, or at least common acquaintance, with everyone who came to the inn. Unusually effusive in manner, his theatrical friendliness was a great comfort to the occidentals who found their way to his door. He had kept his whole staff together, refusing to let anyone go, even during the darkest days of the war when the prospect of survival, let alone of paying guests, was dim indeed. At times the only wages he could offer were a simple servant's closet and whatever the kitchen had that the sparse roster of guests did not eat. But since his own share of the division in those turbulent years was no greater than that of any employee, they did not begrudge him their temporary collective poverty. And when the Turks were gone - letting in a steady flow of Englishmen, Americans and sundry Europeans - he spread his good fortune among them once more. He spoke of them as his kin, and his actions fleshed out these proclamations of loyalty. They returned it in kind without hesitation. Expressionless eyes in stony faces they may have been to passels of foreigners, but behind closed doors they were as joyful and jocular as the best of friends. When two employees, both orphans who had worked with him since childhood, fell in love, he had paid the girl's modest dowry himself, and hosted the wedding at his own expense. This family of servants moved as the limbs of one body, constantly rendering the beauty of the status quo with the predictability of the tides. Yet they were reduced, in the eyes of the officers and the woman, to robed shadows skulking around in corners of the room.

Rugs were lain out in such a pattern as to disguise the tattered edges and threadbare patches. Chairs were simple, but sturdy, generally for the use for the Europeans who had an almost childlike revulsion to sitting on the ground. Lamps burned oil in discrete corners and gave the entire inn a low, pleasant glow. Electricity had been restored in recent years, but it was kept to a minimum in the common areas, shining in full brightness only for the sake of the comfort demanded by westerners in their rooms.

Curios and shelves dating back too long to still be cohesive pieces of furniture had been patched and mended with initially inconsistent scraps of lumber. These shreds of wooden refuse had been repurposed - sculpted, sanded, stained, and fitted - by skills honed over centuries of craftsmanship, a last thread of a dwindling legacy of the natives of this land. As a result, the furniture was not a motley cobbling of castaways, but symphonic harmonies of wood that had been swapped out so many times as to provide a Thesean dilemma to those who were philosophically inclined. None of the foreigners staying at the inn as the new year prepared to begin were disposed to think much along those lines, and took only passing notice of the seemingly useless bric-a-brac that had found perches in shelf and cubby. Useless crumbling pots, stones, frayed cloth faded to the shade of bone by suns that had set many years ago did not hold much interest to them.

Nor were they in the habit of even noticing servants. In the world they inhabited, servants were nameless menials fulfilling their meager capacities by making the life of the able gentry less fraught by the mundane exigencies of the everyday. These creatures were even less worthy of notice than the ones back home who had at least a civilized pedigree and passing understanding of Christian scripture. These were wild desert beasts to most visitors, the particular depravities of their lives irrelevant.

The curly haired officer offered a cigarette to the other and the woman before taking one himself. Striking a match, he lit his own, offered the flame to the woman with a smile, then cocked his eye when the other lieutenant approached and leaned in to grasp the last bit of fire the match had within it.

"I hear the Americans whinging on about not lighting three off a match." Garrett Jameson Townsend, "Townie" to his old friend, delivered the injunction with his customary cheer as he shook out the match.

"Well," Cecil Yap Boyce, the other man, replied stoically. "The Yanks say a lot. It's best not to take them too seriously."

None of the other guests were in the great room of the inn at the moment. They were presumably out at the shops, packing whatever acquisitions they wished to make into the last moments of 1920. The servants scurried here and there like fluttering shades cast by the oil lamps. They scrubbed every corner of every room to an immaculate gleam out of loyalty to a father figure, and the hope of a copper or two from some grateful westerner rather than out of the vestigial fear of the Turkish lash. This slight advance in the station of these threadbare natives was what the British officers would have called their freedom, never letting them forget for a moment that it was a gift from the British.

"I was surprised," Townie said, "to hear that the superstition goes back quite a ways. Crimea was the furthest back anyone knew about it that I've been able to find. Of course, that's not a good way to find out much. Talking to people, I mean."

"Most people haven't much to say," Yap replied. "Doesn't stop them from talking though."

"I think once you've brought it up to someone, they create a memory of it right away. If I were to ask you about a big festival we attended at west end back in aught nine and start describing it to you, then your mind would conjure up the image and start playing it back for you. You would have vivid memories of the carnival, the balloons, the acts we saw. 'Wasn't the organ grinder there with his monkey?' I'd say. You'd search through your memory without realizing it, find an image of an organ grinder, and stick him right in west end, monkey and all, and answer 'Ah, yes. I remember.' Then I would start to think and realize 'No, wait. It wasn't aught nine, that was in thirteen, when I was already stationed in Borneo. Yap couldn't have been there.' But if I didn't say anything to you about it being the wrong year, you'd still think you had actually been there. And you might mention it to someone else who would also start making up memories of the big fair. Then word would spread of the great do of West End in aught nine, even though no such thing had ever come within a mile of happening."

"I'd be a bit more circumspect than that, Townie," Yap said with a smug smile. "I don't think you could convince me that I had been somewhere I hadn't."

"Well, not you specifically, of course, Yap. You've a mind like a steel trap."

"Mmm," Yap agreed without much conviction.

"I just think it's interesting that we can lie to ourselves so easily. I mean, when I ask about no three on a match, I tend to get answers from people about how their grandparents used to say it. Some said that they'd been saying it most of their lives. But then a few fellows even claimed to have invented the idea themselves. Not just claimed it, but had a story behind it. Something to do with the trenches in most cases. But everyone was sure they'd heard it before. And that's strange. It might simply be an American thing."

"Perhaps they made it up to sell something, Garret," Serena, the khaki-clad sister of Yap, offered. "They're awfully keen to do that. If they aren't buying something, I mean."

"Speaking of which," Townie said. "Do you think the others will return soon? The Yanks and all?"

"Does it really matter?" Yap asked. "I mean we could simply get a nice bottle and split it three ways in my room. Do we need to invite half the world to see in the New Year with us?"

"I rather like the idea," Serena said. "People from all over the civilized world, coming together in this little shack in Palestine. Something nice about it."

"Plenty of bleeders from all over the civilized world got together in Flanders a short time ago," Yap observed. "A good time was had by none."

"You are in a foul mood," Serena said.

"Not at all, I'm merely feeling anti-social."

"I hadn't noticed anything different."

"Exactly. I am at my normal degree of being anti-social. And part of me wants to just go to bed right away. Not stay up until the milkman comes round."

"They haven't milkmen here. I don't think."

"Yet another reason to drink a nice dram of brandy and slough off early."

"You're in a terrible mood."

"It's my normal mood."

"Precisely."

"Mmm."

"Well," Townie put forward, "we might want to see what mood the rest of the inn is. Other guests might want an all-night to-do. We wouldn't get much sleep then, eh?"

"With the proper amount of brandy, I think it could be managed."

"Come now, old man. When in Rome."

They were far from old men, of course. Little more than children when they were first in uniform, they had both seen enough of the world to be worn out and to be cured of the curiosity to see much more, even though neither man was quite thirty yet. They'd been friends for too many years to think about, enjoying the most pointless banter as well as Yap's eternal baiting of his sister. Once-impeccable khaki uniforms had become rumpled and wrinkled over the last couple of days, but neither gave a damn. A dash of the unkempt suited both of them, something they couldn't enjoy except on leave in remote corners like this one.

"We're far from Rome. Not that the eternal city is much cleaner these days."

"We can see what our hosts do when midnight comes."

"The Mohammadans don't celebrate much of anything. Merely slink around in robes and steal your billfold."

"You don't fancy living like an Arab? Freedom on the sands. No one but a camel to answer to. Endless sky and landscape so beautiful they could drive you mad."

"I've been driven to madness by too many beautiful things to see the charm in it anymore. And I've no talent for camels, robes and such. It's not the life of an Englishman."

"For some it is."

"Who?"

"Lawrence. You've heard of him."

"Ahh, yes. Gave these blighters their freedom, and they've tried to charge us for the privilege of it. Snookered he was."

"He's a good man."

"Traveling the world making a spectacle of himself. But not too bad for an Oxford man, I suppose."

"If," Townie said, "the Arabs are truly of a mind to take possession of the Levant, I daresay they'll figure out how to do it."

"I think you overestimate their abilities," Yap scoffed.

"How many Arabs are there?" Serena asked.

"No one really knows," Townie answered. "They have a secrecy to them that makes counting difficult. They are also quite mobile when they wish. Bedouins never have any fixed address. Berbers slither in and out of the sea of sand like sharks. Of all the people of this land, we see only the tip of an iceberg."

"And you think they could all mass together?" Serena asked.

"They're more content to kill one another, tribe by tribe, for obscure rights to patches of sand that all look the same to any civilized person," Yap said. "There aren't enough of any particular group to cause any serious trouble, thank God."

"I'm not quite as sanguine as you on that point," Townie countered. "Please bear in mind that during the war the native population was able to finish off the floundering rule of the Turks through small guerrilla actions."

"I would remind you that they had our guidance in said endeavor. I'd be very surprised indeed if one were to find that degree of organization amongst their own number."

"I would not. After working with them, I can tell you that they have a spirit you've not dreamed of. They do have a tendency, however, to put pride before everything, even reason. As a result, they frequently quibble amongst themselves, and no man likes to lay down to the will of another. The best leaven for such a predicament, however, has proven to be a common enemy. They see themselves as family members in righteous quarrels with one another. Something we're none of us strangers to. But if they foresee a threat to the family they will gather around a common banner, I assure you."

"I think you may overestimate their foresight a bit. And even if you're right, what precisely would they be able to do against the might of the European powers? It's one thing to kick a half-dead Turk in the shins, but to actually take on the British Empire? That would be suicidal, and even they can see that."

"Perhaps you're right, my friend. But I would counsel fostering the divisions between them as a far superior, and, I might add, long-term, solution."

"Less costly as well."

"It is at that."

Silence hung gently in the air for a moment while Townie paced, stealing glances at Serena. "Dash it all," Yap said suddenly. "Let's do something. Even if it's wrong, it must be better than bloody nothing."

"Watch your tongue, Cecil," Serena said. "For my sake, if nothing else. You're not in a barracks."

"An officer never finds himself in the barracks," Townie offered. "He always has his own billet. With other officers, on most occasions."

"Where one can swear as much as decency allows," Yap said.

"Decency allows no swearing at all at the moment," Serena said.

"Then I suppose I shall simply remain silent. That suits me."

"Good show," Serena said coldly. Abandoning her stool, she stood up and began to wander. Not following the determined but pointless route of Townie, she strode to the edge of the room, and then floated gently around the perimeter, paying no attention to the actual people in her midst. Instead, her eyes glazed the pillars, walls, and shelves, trying desperately to read deeper meaning into the humbly elegant shapes. They must, she reflected, be indicative of something deeper than the movement of the adze and plane. Looking past the shadows moving about the room, she saw a light in the dining room down a short hallway. Following the lamplight as the magi had the star, she saw there was already a gathering of a half dozen occidentals at the tables, laughing gently. They smiled and waved. She waved back, then walked back to where Yap sat and Townie paced. "Everyone is here," she said. "All the guests are already sitting inside, eating and laughing."

"And drinking, if they've any sense," Yap said.

"And here we've been wondering where everyone had got off to," Townie chuckled. "It's the New Year tonight, and no one had any idea what was happening." He placed another cigarette in his mouth, but before he'd had time to riffle his pockets for a match, an Arab had stepped from the shadows cradling a tiny flame in his fingers. Townie lit his cigarette and reached to search his pockets for a copper when he recognized the face in the orange glow as that of the innkeeper. Whether he had stepped from the shadows or had been one of the faceless swirls of robes tidying the great room, Townie couldn't say. "Oh. Thank you. I was wondering when we'd see you again. Say, we were discussing what you do here to celebrate the New Year?"

"My friends," said the innkeeper. "Not every calendar is the same. Not every year can be tallied by the same passage of a day as the others. To those of my tribe, this is the 20th of Tevet in the year 5681. To our brother sons of Allah, the Hijri Year is 1339 and will not end until September. Yet, in a more meaningful way than calendars, the year begins whenever we wish it. Every day can begin a new year if we wish it to herald rebirth. Every moment can be an entirely new life."

"Exactly," Yap said. "Meaningless numbers. We can hunt up some scotch and call it a night."

"Or," the innkeeper said to the eager Townie, "we can create a celebration this evening. See in the year 1921 if we wish. Or the blessed continuation of 5681. Or of 1339. Or simply gather with friends new and old to appreciate the new day, new year, new life we are celebrating in this very moment."

"How poetic," Serena said. Yap grunted in response.

"So come! Join your new friends in the dining room. And I shall entertain you in the most pleasant style that my humble circumstances allow." Townie, grinning ear to ear, offered his arm to Serena, who took it warmly, and the two strode down the short hallway at the innkeeper's bidding.

Yap stared at the man. "You don't take me in," he said. "I've no patience for your theatrical nonsense. In the absence of any woman not a close relation to me, I'll settle for some scotch and a room that locks from the inside."

"Fear not, my friend. There are women enough inside to make it a pleasant evening indeed."

"All done up in the bed sheets?"

"No, Lieutenant," the innkeeper laughed. "Foreigners as free with their flesh as will please you. And although my dear cousins follow the interdictions of the Prophet - peace be upon him and his descendants - lain against alcohol, I am not so encumbered. You shall find your glass filled as many times as you can drain it."

Yap shrugged. "Not too bad a place. When you come right down to it."

"I cannot offer great luxury. But I can offer my hospitality. I pride myself on pleasing even the most exacting of gentleman."

"I'm not all that exacting," Yap smirked.

"But you have no tolerance for poetic pronouncements or flamboyant behavior. Merely the 'brass tacks', as it were, yes? I am happy to give you what pleases you."

"Well," Yap said, standing and shambling down the hall. "It may be a tolerable evening after all."

The innkeeper bowed gently to him, and then turned to his servants, the family he had gathered together under his roof for so many years. "My friends," he said in gentle Arabic, "please take the rest of the evening off. Celebrate in any way you wish. I shall entertain our guests, of course, but don't let my absence prohibit you from gathering in the spirit of the great father of all of us." The shades stopped their scurrying, and proudly walked, chattering and laughing amongst themselves, restored by the absence of foreigners to the status of humanity once again.

The sole exceptions were the old man, and the woman in the niqab, who stayed at their perch near the door.

"Please," the innkeeper said. "Rest."

"I think it better that we work," the man responded.

"All things have their season. Play as well as work."

"Poverty runs through the year. I am here by your charity, and I will not forget it. All of the mighty fall. Mark my words, there will be great snows soon. And but for you I would be out in them. Better that I should be dead than to watch my lands so defiled. Perhaps I should be out in the cold, when the snows come."

"Fear not, my liege," the innkeeper told the old man, who began to weep again. "We are together tonight. Until your lands are restored to you, you are my royal guest."

"I am not royal anymore," the old man responded. "I am no one's liege lord anymore. None of this," he said, waving at the trinkets on the shelves, "means anything any longer. I am a beggar. The only reason I am not on the street is your kindness."

"If you feel you must lay apart your title until you are restored, then so be it. But it is not pity which keeps you beneath my roof. If you will not see it as my duty, then see it as the love I can extend to a friend."

The woman in the niqab - the last princess of the royal house whose name had been all but forgotten in the scuffling grasp of the lands and the dissolution of ancient bloodlines - walked up to her father and laid a hand on his. He took no affront at her familiarity, clasping her fingers loosely. "I begin to doubt that I shall ever be restored. Allah has willed that I die penniless with no kingdom, my sons' blood all spent in the fruitless struggle not to lose it."

"It will be my pleasure to see you restored, to see our lands and our people back in the hands of their rightful shepherd. To see these relics back in the palace," the innkeeper said, gesturing to the objects resting on the shelf. "To kneel before you as my king."

"You, my friend, are far too noble in spirit to kneel before anyone."

"Majesty must be honored."

"Not these days," the old king said, looking out at the night. "I had a vision of the great wall covered in snow. I saw these Britons standing atop drifts that had all but covered those ancient stones, final conquerors of this land."

"Nothing is final, my old friend. Snows melt."

The old king smiled, and squeezed his daughter's rough, overworked fingers gently before letting go. His hands had found true joy in dragging clean rags over the walls and floors and bringing away dust and grime. More than the men they had slain in battle, more than the might they'd punctuated while being held aloft when their owner made some royal proclamation in his tent that would affect the lives of thousands, more than the feel of the robes of silk in the old days, his hands enjoyed cleaning this little corner of the world even if they grew as dirty and calloused as a slave's in the process. His daughter was staring up at the moon, perhaps trying to imagine what it would look like against the snows of the blizzards to come.

The innkeeper let go of his true smile, breathed deeply, settled into the geniality he used for the foreigners with the skill of an accomplished actor, and strode down the hall to the dining room.

SENECIDE - CHAPTER ONE

CHRISTMAS IN NEW YORK

JOYCE deCORDOVA

It could have been the inspiration for a Norman Rockwell painting. There was the Hutchinson family on Christmas day gathered around a table decorated with candles and holly. Although in short supply and expensive, a ham with all the fixings was in the center plus a decanter of cider, some wine and apple pie to make the dinner complete. There were Jake and Margaret, parents and grandparents to two children and three grandchildren. All had their heads bowed in prayer giving thanks for the blessings they had and asking for the strength to brave what lay ahead. They all knew this was to be their last Christmas together.

For the past ten years, the United States and the rest of the planet witnessed the earth spiraling towards destruction. Famine was now rampant in two thirds of the world. Water supply was dangerously low and depleting the earth, the scorching sun mercilessly pounding out its heat and destroying everything in its path. New technologies were in the making but not coming quickly enough to supply the necessary resources for the more than the 10 billion people inhabiting the earth in this year of 2050.

Rather than bringing the planet together, this fight for survival - because that is what it was - a new, yet old policy resurged in the United States. It went back to Isolationism, a newer version of the Monroe Doctrine. By a wide margin, it was agreed that protectionism, save what is left, became one of the answers to survival. Our technology was the most sophisticated in the world and, because of this and because there was a prototype now used by Australia, it was able to design a wide and so far impenetrable force field around its borders. Australia had decided on the ring more than 5 years ago and that nation was thriving. Because of their distance and configuration, isolation was not a great issue and the Australians overwhelming voted for the "bubble". However, the configuration of the US was different and more complicated. States such as Alaska and Hawaii that were not connected were given a time frame of 6 months to either secede from the nation or immigrate to the States. Many chose the former and then the deed was done. It was decided that the force field would be revaluated after 5 years. Physically, no one was allowed in or out. Yes, there was communication between the countries, minimal at best, but the more knowledge we had of the plight of other nations, the more we knew this was the right thing to do. Take care of our own and then, if there was anything left, we could extend ourselves, but not until we were secure and our resources were replenished and safe.

However, although sensible, isolationism was not enough and so in 2050 a radical and unprecedented decision was made to try and save ourselves. It was unanimously decided by the government that those over the age of 70 needed to be "removed" or, more delicately phrased, they were to "move on". For humankind to continue, they had to make the ultimate sacrifice.

The logic to this decision was: Many of the elderly were being kept alive with expensive medications, chemotherapy, pacemakers, artificial hearts, transplanted kidneys and lungs, robotic limbs - but for what purpose? They were expendable. If the planet were to survive, were not the young the only hope?

This directive, although harsh, was not a total surprise to Jake & Margaret. They had been expecting it since the late teens of the millennium. The first directive came in 2025. It stated that only palliative care was to be offered to those over 80. But, as resources became scarce, economic and social pressures lowered the palliative care age to 75. Then in 2050, as we were gasping our last, and the aged because of their huge numbers and lower birth rates, demanding and receiving more care and comforts, the radical decree was made and measures were taken to see that it was enforced. No more complicated surgeries meant to keep them alive & well beyond a hundred years. No longer were the young to be their caretakers and forced to exist in the constant heat, grateful for their pittance of water and food. The planet was becoming unbearable as it continued to spiral towards destruction and the young were becoming increasingly resentful and angry, almost to the point of blaming the elderly for daring to be old, as if this was their idea and they became weaker and more physically and mentally more feeble on purpose. The Inuits had the right idea: Put them on an ice flow and good riddance! Certainly the young did not seek their wisdom. What wisdom? How could you speak about life if you couldn't communicate with 21st century tools? The graybeards had given up understanding the new technologies. As soon as they learned to operate something, a new and better and faster version would replace it. And why bother when you had all these young people you could hire and make it happen? Conversation between generations had virtually stopped. The old were annoyed and confused listening to the young speaking in acronyms. They just couldn't relate to not hearing full sentences anymore. On the other hand, the young were frustrated by the slow pace of their speech and the long descriptions and time it would take an old man to say something that they could say in a nano-second. So the young dismissed them as having no consequence in their lives except eating up the planet that rightfully should belong to them.

This was the undeniable fact: The population was overwhelmingly gray and, with each old person using up resources, the threat of annihilation of the young and thereby the country's future became more of a reality. The old were destroying any chance for the country to survive, and therein lay the heart of the matter.

The deadline of January First was fast approaching. Both at 85, neither Grandfather Jake nor Grandmother Margaret would be welcoming in the New Year of 2051. So the Hutchinson family joined hands one more time. They embraced each other and ate the dinner as best they could. Practical matters such as wills, estates, belongings had already been discussed and decided. They focused on the good times, about family vacations and the time when grandma forgot to put her teeth in and scared the little ones, or when Charlotte, then aged 5, got drunk at a party because everyone was giving her a sip of their wine. It was these small events that brought a chuckle and a smile.

JAKE AND MARGARET

Jake and Margaret were given pills by KARMA, the United States division in charge of the project, or, as it was defined, in charge of The Transition. KARMA was no acronym; the name was symbolic. The fate of the universe was on the shoulders of those 70 plus. This "transition" for the sake of others was their fate. The depleting of resources was man's doing and now the saving of what was left was in their hands. It was their mission. When they were given the pills, a chip was placed at the base of their skull to signal KARMA when the deed was done. Their bodies would disintegrate. They would leave no trace. The country did not have the resources to bury the dead or even take care of the ashes. Funeral parlors had literally "died out" in about 2030 when the economy was tumbling and the focus was on saving the living. The pills were to be taken before the first...at their leisure, so to speak. There would be no pain, only a cloud of numbness eventually stopping their hearts. Jake and Margaret told the family they would do this in the privacy of their own room.

Margaret was wracked with a mixture of emotions. She was a nurturer and, intellectually, she believed that the country was dying and the huge number of graying baby boomers was one of the major causes. The image of babies being born in Africa, into a world with little food and very little water, was now closer to home. In fact, it was home. Babies with swollen bellies and huge eyes were becoming more frequent and, just by being alive, she felt it was partly her fault and "moving on" was a logical solution.

She was a tall woman, "lean and long" her mother used to say. Her hair cascaded down her back. It was straight with becoming streaks of gray she never bothered to color. She had the body of a ballerina even at 85. Ramrod straight, and yet she exuded a languidness, an ethereal quality that people found calming. Her eyes were her most striking feature. They were large and round, the color of dark chocolate and age had not diminished their intensity. At 85, thanks to modern medicine, she was healthy. Her knees and hips had been replaced; her heart was pumping beautifully since her surgery and would last at least another 50 years. Dementia and arthritis had been cured and were no longer a threat. She also felt a sense of purpose in life. She had decided to volunteer as a nurse. She believed she was useful and needed. She also believed in the innate goodness of her fellow man and, if just given the right direction or opening, that would prove to be true. Throughout her life, she tried to provide that. So, being a trusting and, at times, naïve sort of woman, and one who always obeyed the law and trusted her government to do the right thing, she understood why she was classified as expendable. Her classification made sense, and yet, she did not totally embrace it.

Margaret had an uneasy feeling that maybe this whole project KARMA wasn't about saving the country, but about power. This uneasiness was due to Jake. During their more than sixty years of life together, Margaret relied on him for the street smarts that he had. Jake's gut was never wrong. He knew when something just didn't add up, didn't smell right, and she trusted him.

From the time he could remember, Jake embraced danger as part of what made him who he was. Danger was a constant in his life. His intuitive alertness & response to it was one of the reasons that he, at 85 years old, was alive and well in 2050.

Father coming at him with a strap; bullies with bats and chains in the schoolyard; combat soldier in Afghanistan. His body told the map of his life. He was tall, though slightly stooped. His upper body was lean and held up by legs that were a tangle of gnarled veins. The tip of the third finger of his left hand had been sliced off by a bayonet during combat. His father's beatings (for what reason?) had left scars on his back and buttocks, and his nose was broken by a rifle butt. Men respectfully steered clear of him, but women found him handsome in an ugly sort of way.

Although very different in temperament in approaching life and people, one thing they did have in common was pride. Jake and Margaret didn't want their family to see them gasping their last.

They told the family they didn't want to traumatize them. They told them that death for them was to be a private matter. That is what they told them. That is not what they did.

After Christmas dinner and poignant goodbyes, Jake and Margaret went to their room and pulled their knapsacks out from under the bed. They were to travel light - very light. A change of clothes, lots of cash, first aid kit, their new phones which were untraceable and self charging and their cache of lasers, guns and knives. Disarming the chip was complicated, but Jake had been secretly educating himself for months with a cohort of his and easily removed Margaret's. She, although nervous and trembling, finally removed his. He then programmed the chips to relay a message to KARMA that the deed was done. They were gone, vaporized with no trace. They then rappelled from their window and stealthy walked away in the bitter cold towards a safe house.

Some of the elderly went quietly into the night, but then there were those like Jake and Margaret, members of ANTIQUUM; a covert organization whose members believed their mission was to find, capture and destroy the enemy. They believed that the elimination of the elderly was only the beginning. Next would be the disabled, the blind and the deaf; many of them young and in need of constant care. They believed that there was a conspiracy among the powers to slowly, methodically and insidiously shape the country to the way they wanted it. To the way they could control it. It was all about power, not saving the country.

The members of ANTIQUUM were five million strong. They had wisdom and they had money. Jake had been a fighter all his life. He was resilient and he was one of the most important operatives in ANTIQUUM. Until they could convince people that the "suicides" would not stop with just the elderly, that other groups would follow and be forced to "move on", the enemy was any adult under seventy.

Finding and routing out the enemy however was not easy. Who were they? Fearing the "transition", many over seventy had face-lifts and body sculpting and looked much younger than their years. And, to complicate matters, some of those who looked old were not. Drugs and alcohol had given many of them a wasted aged look. Knowing this, KARMA had devised a portable scanner that had 100% eye recognition. There was a group of KARMA troopers who would go on surprise missions throughout the United States, round up a group of citizens and quietly gather those over seventy - never to be seen again.

The night was bitter cold. It was the wind that did it. It sliced right through you and made you gasp. People were folding into themselves and fighting to keep their eyes open as much as possible. Cold brings tears and tears blur your vision. That could mean danger for Jake and Margaret.

Christmas in New York was magical, but January was bleak, gray and ominous and the look of January matched the mood for what lay ahead of them

ACCIDENTS WILL HAPPEN

JEAN SCHWEIBISH

I moved through most of my childhood in a constant kinetic state, frequently bumping into, tripping over, or tangling in the animate and inanimate with willful abandon. An astonishing ratio of falls amassed as time went on. My father, always the kind of person to put a positive spin on things, would tell people I was his adventurous daughter, or sometimes simply that I was such an active kid the occasional mishap was bound to occur. He never referred to me as clumsy or careless, and he was saddened by the clever cruelty of some of the kids in my school who liked to say I had "down syndrome."

I find it nearly impossible to conjure up a time during those years when I *didn't* have scraped knees or elbows, cuts or bruises and even the occasional chipped tooth. Black and blue marks were a source of pride, and stitches - well, stitches were medals of honor. Nothing ever stopped me from heading off to explore the world, especially anything as familiar as falling down.

My father would kid me about "my adventures" as I grew up but not out of the mishaps. "You'd be a great stuntwoman for the movies!" he'd boom at me. I'd smile back and say "I'll give you my autograph," and we'd both laugh. After each incident, however, behind a closed bedroom door at night my father would have a thunderously serious argument with my mother. I'd once asked her about these arguments, and she'd scoffed and said, "We don't argue, we have loud discussions." The loud discussions apparently always ended when my father would finally blame my mother for my latest injury. Not a peep could be heard from their second floor bedroom, and I knew the discussion was at an end by their silence. The bedroom door would open, light spilling into the hall and down the stairs where I sometimes sat straining my ears to hear what was being said and if it was about me. Like clockwork in the next day or two my mother would come to me and tell me what my Dad had said to her.

"You don't think I'm the reason for your mishaps, do you, Maggie?" she always asked.

How could she possibly be responsible for my mishaps, I always wondered. The question made little sense to me. But somehow I understood that my mother needed my reassurance that she played no part in the accidents, and each time I cobbled together some sort of offering. Once I actually suggested that I was just naturally accident prone, and compared my constant tumbles to the way my older sister Claire's hair was straight and thick while mine was curly and fine. "It's just the way we were made I guess," I'd said, finishing my explanation *du jour* with what I thought was my most winning smile. She had looked at me for a long moment, studying my face to see if I was serious, assumed I really believed what I'd just told her, and reached out to wrap me in a tight hug.

"You'll grow out of it," she had assured me.

I very much doubted that, but had kept the thought to myself.

* * * * * * * * * * *

To try to pinpoint where this all began, I'd say it had to be my first day of school. My mother had taken a full-time job to help with household bills, which meant there would be no one home to tend me all day. Arrangements were made without any input from me, but who discusses such things with a 3 year old? The place I was finally enrolled in is termed "pre-school" these days, but then it was simply "nursery school." Pre-school puts a more positive spin on children under the age of five spending a whole day away from their mothers. Nursery school tells it like it is - or was.

The brief time spent at nursery school still conjures up a potent mixture, a kaleidoscope of the sounds of other kids' voices, the smells of paper towels and liquid soap, iodine and a freshly opened Band-Aid, the excitement of learning games like *duck, duck, goose* with kids my age and making friends for the first time, the routines of milk and cookies and nap time, the sleepy start and weary end of each day. No one in my family, least of all me, had a clue how my life would change for anything but the better. But it was the first time anyone can recall my problem with staying upright. And to this day I still harbor how my three-year-old self felt on the very first day, like I'd spent it falling down a long flight of stairs in slow motion.

It's funny how one remembers certain things from childhood with such crystalline clarity. For me it's such things as the circus atmosphere of the Howdy Doody wallpaper on my nursery walls, my throwing my bottle out of the crib in jealousy as I watched my big sister drink out of a grownup cup, the feeling of frustration over being trapped in a playpen in our front yard while the big kids were running around having fun. And, of course, there's that first day of nursery school, a little herky-jerky movie projected through my mind's eye.

The opening begins with the morning of that first day. My mother, usually so unaffected by time and always so attentive to my demands, seemed a total stranger. Lost in herself, she had rushed me through my breakfast, giving me a wide berth, instead of sitting down with me as usual. I later came to realize she had on her work clothes, and kept her distance to protect them from my less than tidy eating habits. That morning she wore a string of imitation pearls which had caught my attention and my desire, and I reached out to grab them just as she put my juice down in front of me. Instead of the usual smiling face and hands quick to distract with a favorite toy, I was jolted by a loud "No!" and the first look of anger I'd ever seen on her familiar face.

It had been raining that day, and my breakfast abruptly over I was set down on the floor to have boots put on. At some prior time, perhaps on a particularly difficult day, my mother must have whispered in conspiratorial fashion that we were going to hide my toes from everyone, as a way to coax me into my shoes. She was always clever in her choices to distract me and conquer any potential objections on my part. There was no stopping me, once I understood the game. It was just as much fun to free them all on my own, and I would gladly have played the hide and find game all day. But on this morning, it seemed my mother had forgotten the game. Instead, she seemed to still harbor anger for my seeming indifference to some undisclosed timetable. She forced the boots onto my unsuspecting feet and I, of course, balked. The confusion over what was going on, why my favorite person was treating me as she was, and why I wasn't allowed to play my favorite game was just too much to comprehend. I began to cry and I kicked at her.

"Stop this now, Maggie! Be a big girl," my mother had said. "Mommy hasn't hurt you and we're in a hurry today - no time for playing games."

Puzzled, I must have wondered what it meant that there was no time for playing games. What else was there in my universe to do while awake?

Having succeeded in getting my boots on over my struggles, my mother had gone to get my coat and hat off the wall pegs in the entrance hall. To me this was a clear sign that the game should finally begin and I had my boots off and a triumphant smile ready for her when she came back into the kitchen.

"Margaret!" my mother had snapped. "What a bad girl you're being this morning! You're making Mommy late!"

That wiped the smile right off my face. A kind of anxious feeling planted a small seed in me that morning. I had no idea who this loud, angry person was even though she looked like my mother. I finally wised up that something was wrong in the world I knew and sat still while the rain boots were forced onto my feet again. Game over, I offered no further struggles against my mother's distracted and hurried movements as she then pushed my arms into the sleeves of my coat, tied my hat on, and adjusted the brim on it so she could look into my eyes. She chucked me under the chin and said "that's better," and gave me a small quick hug before she went back out of the room for her own coat and hat.

The kitchen scene fades and my mother and I are traveling in the family's station wagon. That would've been a treat to me in those days, yet something that morning hadn't felt right. First of all, it had always been my father behind the big wheel of the car, and he hadn't been at home that morning. Unable to puzzle this out, I became distracted by a memory of another car trip, this one with the whole family as usual. That trip had been very unlike our typical boisterous outings with my father teasing my mother into singing and all of us joining along in one fashion or another - Dad in his deep off-key manner, Claire in her high-pitched giggly tone, Mother in her lovely soprano, and me, echoing their words in a lisped and garbled fashion. That other trip had been a long one, and I'd slept through most of it from the motion of the car, the warmth of my family and the silence during the drive. A movie within a movie remains with me to this day; an impression of an endless sea of dark skirts and pants swirling slowly about in a large and dimly lit room. Many unfamiliar voices, all soft, hushed. My father picking me up to introduce me to some solemn, unsmiling female faces, upon which I hide my own face in his neck. Something triggered these memories as my mother buckled me into my car seat, and I yawned in her face.

"Take a nap, honey," my mother encouraged. "We'll be there in no time." *Where?* I wondered as I heard the car start, and slowly nodded off.

The 'where' turned out to be the Hobby Horse Nursery School in front of which my mother had just parked our car as I opened my eyes. Out the window I saw a large, white farmhouse with a bright red front door, and two ladies standing side by side in the front yard, apparently waiting for us. There was a white picket fence surrounding the property and corralling an oversized rocking horse. The two ladies were dressed similarly in dark, full skirts, cheerful floral print blouses, and dark cardigans draped across their shoulders. They also both wore bright smiles, beamed in our direction. The tall thin one, Miss Fran, as I learned to call her, gave a little wave to us.

My mother opened the back door of our car and leaned in to release me from my car seat.

"You'll like it here Maggie. You'll meet other children, and I think Miss Fran and Miss Clara are very nice ladies," she had whispered, more like she was reassuring herself rather than telling me something I needed to know.

A surefooted toddler, I promptly scrambled my way out of the car seat and on to whatever adventure my mother had planned for us. She appeared to like the two smiling ladies, and she had somehow stopped being that stranger who had shouted at me earlier. The big, red hobbyhorse on the lawn matched my rain boots. The sun had decided to peak out of the clouds and join us. The day was brightening up. My mother took hold of my hand and we headed up the brick walk to where the shorter of the two women swung open a gate and welcomed us.

"Good morning!" she chirped. "So good to see you again Mrs. Davis. And you must be Margaret," she added, as she smiled down at me.

Brave and adventurous child that I'd been not one minute before, I stared at the woman holding her hand out to me and promptly hid my face in my mother's coat.

"Don't be shy, Maggie. Miss Clara is a new friend. She isn't going to bite you!" my mother said, and laughed.

I poked my head out, looked up at my mother and then directed a careful smile at Miss Clara. She returned the smile and offered her hand again.

"We have some nice things to play with in the back yard Margaret - or shall we call you Maggie? Would you like to see them? Swings and monkey bars and a slide!"

By then Miss Fran had joined us to shake hands with my mother and she too was smiling down at me. I still had hold of my mother's hand, but I began to relax. I liked Miss Fran's red hair and Miss Clara's voice sounded like music to me.

"Miss Fran," said Miss Clara, "meet Maggie. Maggie, this is Miss Fran. We're heading off to see the swings in the backyard, right Maggie?"

I looked up at my mother again and she nodded 'yes' at me, released my hand and stroked my hair.

"Go on ahead Maggie." she had said softly.

I took hold of Miss Clara's proffered hand and we headed off. I looked back over my shoulder during most of that journey to make sure my mother was still there, and she was, smiling at me as she talked with Miss Fran. As we went around the corner of the house and I could no longer catch sight of my mother when I looked back, I began to anticipate what I was about to see. Miss Clara told me about the other little girls and boys who would be coming to join me on the slide, the monkey bars and the swings, and the games we'd learn to play together. The back yard was as wonderful as had been described. I was thrilled with the red swing set, the yellow slide and the monkey bars, and couldn't wait to try them out.

"Time to go back and join Miss Fran, Maggie, so we can greet the other mommies and your new friends who'll be arriving any minute now," Miss Clara said.

I couldn't wait to tell my mother about the wonderful things in the backyard, or to see who my new friends would be, so I eagerly clasped Miss Clara's hand and followed.

As we came back around the corner of the house I first spotted a little boy with a chubby woman I took to be his mother talking to Miss Fran. My eyes searched frantically for *my* mother. A brown car was parked where our blue station wagon had been. All I saw in front of me was the red-haired, thin Miss Fran talking to a dark-haired lady clutching the hand of a scowling, straining, dark-haired kid. He apparently had more sense than I did. He was determinedly pulling in the direction of their car and nearly knocked his mother off her feet in his efforts.

Miss Clara momentarily let go of my hand to straighten her cardigan before approaching the new arrivals. In a panic, I began to run towards the gate, towards the street, towards - what? Who? My mother had disappeared! As I ran under a large, old shade tree I caught my booted foot on a gnarled root and went flying.

Miss Clara came running, as did Miss Fran and even the dark-haired mommy who scooped up her protesting son and hurried towards me. I was surprised and left a bit breathless, but I didn't cry. Nothing was broken, the Misses Clara and Fran agreed, after they had looked me over. They smiled up at the lady with the squirming son with some embarrassment, picked me up, dusted me off and introduced me to the newcomers.

"Maggie has seen our swings and slide and monkey bars Bobby, wouldn't you like to see them too?" asked Miss Fran.

"No!" yelled Bobby.

His mother looked apologetically at the two women then at her son and said: "See how good Maggie is being Bobby? Why don't you show her how good *you* can be?"

"Won't!" shouted little Bobby.

I remember Bobby as quite the savvy kid. We became good friends over the years. He was one of the few kids who never gave me grief about my falls, he'd just give me a hand up and dust me off like he'd seen the Misses Clara and Fran do so many times during our time at the Hobby Horse.

The rest of that day was a blur of ups and downs. I fell off my stool during milk and cookies. I hit my head on a low branch in the back yard while running around with the other kids and fell back onto my rear end. I slipped on the steps going into the house for lunch and fell off my cot after lunch as I tried to reach over to a newfound friend during naptime. In retelling it all these years later, it sounds funny, like a silent film era slapstick comedy, but I still know that was the longest, hardest day I'd experienced in my short life, getting hurt with no Mommy to comfort me. Miss Fran and Miss Clara tried, but there were seven other kids in their care and since I never cried or made a fuss, they thought everything was under control. And in a way they were right.

At the end of that first day - and it had been a long day as I'd been the first to arrive in the morning and the last to leave (a routine that became standard) - I was one weary kid.

It was with great disbelieving relief that I spotted my mother pulling up in front of the nursery school. I'd been told, as had all the kids, that our mothers would see us at the end of our day and we'd have much to share. It was hard to understand the concept of time as I was experiencing it and I no longer felt like I was ever going to go home, much less tell my mother about my day. Miss Fran quietly talked to my mother while Miss Clara got me into my coat and hat. The image of my mother looms like a close-up, her eyes searching my face for telltale signs of the wear and tear my body had absorbed that day as she picked me up to take me out to the car. She kissed my cheek and I rested my head on her shoulder as she walked away from the big white house with the red front door, and down the brick walk we had traveled up such a long time ago. She buckled me in my car seat, told me to close my eyes, and that we'd be home before I knew it. No encouragement had been necessary. I had closed my eyes and was out cold, the scene naturally fading to black.

The next thing I knew I was home, in my bed, hearing the murmur of voices and the smell of dinner. It was dark by then and I felt afraid at first until I could make out the sound of my father's rising voice and my mother shushing him. I climbed out of bed, grabbed a favorite stuffed animal and headed for the voices.

Rubbing my eyes with my remaining free hand, I walked into the kitchen in time for a collision with my father, who had just turned as I entered and was on his way to wake me up for dinner. Down I went. This time the tears started to trickle down my face. It had been a very long day and this was the last straw. I had no more energy left to keep control of my feelings.

"Oh, Maggie-baby, I'm so sorry!" my Dad exclaimed. "Mommy was telling me what a hard day you had and I go and make it even harder!" With this he picked me up, cradled me and walked into the living room.

"Time for dinner!" my mother called after us.

"Dinner will wait a little," my father replied, as he sat down in his favorite chair and dabbed at my tears with his handkerchief. "Margaret and I need to have a conference."

"But I'm hungry!" my sister whined from her place at the kitchen table.

Claire, always a good sister to me, later understood the point of my father's conferences with me, but interfere with her meal schedule, and you'd hear about it. She still gets cranky if she doesn't eat on time, but we know it's a blood-sugar issue these days, and so was never quite in her control.

My mother continued to work; our family needed the two incomes to get by. Nursery school had been a necessity for the two years before I entered kindergarten. I somehow understood this, and that she hadn't chosen a job over me. She didn't have much left to give me at the end of her day, and often apologized for not being able to stay awake as she read to me before bedtime.

Over the years I broke various bones, sprained one ankle or the other a few times and had numerous occasions for stitches. Although my parents never failed to comfort me, most of the time they weren't around when the accidents happened. My father's conferences with me found us discussing all kinds of things as years passed. Sometimes he'd bring up the stuntwoman idea or some other high-risk activity, like racecar driver. Sometimes we'd get into comparisons of past accidents. Sometimes he would simply ask if I had these accidents on purpose to give him premature grey hair, and then tug at one of my pigtails. Eventually he'd always ask, very quietly, "What's bothering you, Maggie?"

I didn't usually know what to answer my father and often just lifted a shoulder and my eyebrows in mute reply. Most of the time I honestly had no clue; it had just been one of those days when life tripped me up. As with my mother, I could feel my father wanted some sort of explanation that made sense to him, so I'd offer whatever came to mind - something about schoolwork, a teacher, a quarrel with one of my friends. But mostly I replied with silent body language.

It never failed that within a day or two of one of my father's conferences with me, my mother would have a heart-to-heart with me. Always the same question - was it something that involved her? Was it because I'd been sick and had to stay at home alone? Was it because she'd been too tired to read to me the night before? Was it because she'd gotten out of work later than usual and had to pick me up late from my friend's house, where I stayed after school? I always rushed to deny that whatever accident I'd just had had anything to do with her, and I never told my father about the heart-to-hearts he pushed her into - maybe because I subconsciously wanted each of them to think she *was* to blame; maybe because I liked the idea that sometimes, when I wasn't around, they were thinking and talking about me.

I used to wonder if my sister ever got her thoughts so stirred up. I finally concluded it was unlikely since Claire never had "problems with gravity" - her description to her friends on the subject of my falls and her gentle way of teasing me. The only time she ever fell was when I dared her to catch me as I ran off with her favorite book. I had waited around the corner of the house and as she came around, stuck my foot out and down she went. I had laughed and briefly felt pretty good to be the upright sister for a change, but that quickly morphed into guilt and I felt ashamed. Later, when my parents heard the story from Claire, who thought this a cheap shot on my part and therefore she'd been duty-bound to tell them about it, I was mortified to hear my father's reproving tone as he informed me this had been the meanest thing I could have done to anyone, much less my own sister. "You of all people should know how crummy it is to take a tumble!" he'd said, sadness in his eyes. Dessert was off the menu for me that night, but that was no great punishment compared to the look on my father's face and the disappointment in his voice. He had always been my ally and I had let him down.

"Apologize to your sister, then go to your room and really think about what you did to Claire," he had said, sternly shaking his head in displeasure.

Red-faced, I had mumbled "I'm sorry, Claire" and with downcast eyes fled the table for the solace of my favorite stuffed animal, and an abundance of hot, remorseful tears.

Two days later, as I helped my mother hang the wash, we had an unusual heart-to-heart. My mother looked very sadly at me, but I had nothing to reassure her with. All I could say was that I'd made a big mistake and I was really sorry; it would never happen again. For a long time after the incident it continued to bother me that I'd tripped Claire. She'd always been good to me, not like some of my friends' older siblings, and it wasn't her fault that gravity wasn't such a challenge for her. It bothered me far longer to think about the things my parents might've said about me in their discussion the night of the incident with my sister. I would conjure up my father's face at the dinner table, and my mother's face during our heart-to-heart and the tears would well up. The prank was never again brought up by either of my parents, or by my sister, for which I was grateful. It was a small lesson in the grand scheme of things but a lesson learned. I never pulled a stunt like that in my life again, not on anyone.

* * * * * * * * * * * *

All of this comes flooding back to me now as I gaze at my daughter, Olivia, who sits across the kitchen table from me, spooning oatmeal carefully into her mouth. She's doing her best to avoid spilling on her new pink sweater with imitation pearl buttons. It's raining today, and we plan to sit side by side on the hall bench to put on our boots "like big girls." She is very excited to be going to school for the first time and has spoken of nothing but school all week. Each time I've looked inquiringly at my husband as she projects what school will be like, in her high-pitched but serious voice, and later, behind closed bedroom doors, we discuss again whether this is the right thing for Olivia. She's a very different child than I was at her age, and the times are very different too, we both agree. However, I still can't help but ponder with a weight on my heart, what her first day at pre-school will be like, and what movie she'll carry with her for the rest of her life.

Voyeur

Kit Storjohann

As I stared through the window, studying Mrs. Glatz in her bath, I let out a trembling breath that combined my exhilaration with the relief that the moment justified all of the preparation I had put into it. For weeks I had observed that Mrs. Glatz's tub was being filled at the same time every night. The rattling in the pipes behind the walls of my room heralded the disrobing and immersion of a female body, a mysterious fully-grown woman living within the house. It had stirred feelings in my pre-adolescent self that hadn't yet found the right words or release. I had discovered – through discrete glances from the yard with the pretext of kicking around a soccer ball – that her bathroom window was always open with the blinds up. The window was directly above the tub; even a boy of my age could see directly in if positioned properly behind the little hillock in the yard. And I had made certain that I was positioned properly, that my timing was absolutely perfect.

When Mrs. Glatz had first moved in, my initial response was bubbling resentment that my freedom at night would be restrained. Even at that age I was a night owl. My nocturnal activities went completely undetected due to the fact that my bedroom was on the ground floor, while my parents slept upstairs. As they'd had me late in their lives my birth had not been planned, and the upstairs rooms had all settled into functions already. My parents' role in my life had been more

97

like an aunt and uncle, and they granted me a great deal of latitude in my activities. In their eyes, there was no reason why a boy couldn't sleep on the ground floor of his own home. The nights that I'd spent cowering from monsters and other unspeakable threats of the darkness when I was younger with no reinforcements a shout away had given me a sense of self-reliance that none of my classmates seemed to have. Their avuncular role extended to their daily lives in the town as well. Many parents of my classmates – assuming from my parents' advanced ages that I was the last of a larger brood – thought that they had been through all of the worries and insecurities before, and looked to them for advice. My mother and father always did their best to answer questions, couching their vague responses in general philosophical terms with beginnings like "I have generally found ..." This, combined with their almost inexhaustible patience, gave them an air of sagacity and an unofficial capacity of wise elders.

In accordance with their improvised wisdom, I was largely left to my own devices. When I couldn't sleep, I had free reign to amuse myself. Throughout much of the year, I corralled my substitutes for sleep into silent games in which I challenged absent friends, playing for both of us. I inevitably found a way to best whoever I was contesting as he lay asleep, blissfully unaware of his defeat. A series of games of strategy played on invisible boards with ever-mutating rules were my preferred method of whiling away the stagnant hours of darkness. The world was conquered hundreds of times in the form of imaginary tokens on hypothetical maps. I had no interest in reading or mulling over the day's failure like most insomniacs. Reading tended to lose its charm as the night wore on. In accordance with old habits, rather than any specific belief, my parents had no television in the house, so that particular mindless distraction was not a possibility.

Left to the whims of my own mind, I would end up having conversations with the friends I was playing against. Although I would not actually respond for them, I would continue the conversation by surmising their response. These discussions would often become heated. More often than not, they would end with me rampaging against some injustice I did not understand. Half-informed ideas about the unfair nature of the world and the ubiquitous capricious authority of adults fueled my rants, and another person on the ground floor could not help but notice it. My mother had discretely inquired about how I slept on a few mornings following nights that had found her visiting the kitchen in the middle of the night for one reason or another.

When the darkness began to retreat in both directions each day and the night air was content to gently envelop a wanderer with a palpable but pleasant chill, I frequently found myself exploring the few blocks which made up the boundaries of my world. In other towns - ones I imagined as havens for people like me based on their descriptions in books - I might well have encountered company on my restless journey through the nights of my childhood. My hometown, however, was early to sleep and early to rise in accordance with its aspirations. I would walk in circles around my neighborhood, trying unsuccessfully to convince myself that this place I was consigned to was interesting enough that I could discover something new each time I took the time to look at it. Scenes were played out in my head of the goings on of the places in town that I passed. These ranged from the banal activities of everyday exchanges to more scandalous speculations of the druggist secretly providing narcotics to our shaky-handed doctor and to the fantastic scenarios of sudden invasion by aliens or communists.

Before Mrs. Glatz's arrival, the announcement was made at supper one evening that our noisier nighttime activities would have to be tabled in deference to our new boarder. My parents tended to couch disciplinary orders in the guise of suggestions of general self-improvement. They had not wanted to take in a lodger, and had done so merely as a favor to the principal of the school where she would begin work in the fall. The story of how a woman from out of town came to be living with us was revealed to me in dribs and drabs in my parents' conversations with each other, as well as shreds of gossip I'd filched from adults when they thought my ears were closed; never through questioning the lodger herself.

According to my investigations, Mrs. Glatz had left her teaching position in a different part of the state when she married. Mr. Glatz's early death, from a disease which remained mysterious from his first deep cough to his funeral, produced an attractive young widow with an enchanting darkness about her. Embarking upon a new life, Mrs. Glatz returned to teaching, but chose to do so hundreds of miles from everything she found familiar. Rather than remain the young Widow Glatz, she left her hometown to become someone other than the poor girl that everyone had seen grow up, teach their children, marry, and mourn. My parents quietly thought it somewhat odd that she would choose to be a stranger rather than wait for the next available beau to give her a new last name, but it made perfect sense to me.

Arriving on one of the darkest days of winter, she had accepted a position at the school which would not begin until the afternoon light began to fade again the following fall. Her affairs from her old life were put in order, her house sold, and most of her possessions given away. She moved into our spare room in the late spring to await the commencement of her employment and seek a home of her own. Summer found me wandering the neighborhood at night, as I couldn't risk verbalizing world conquest or a one-sided argument with only a wall between Mrs. Glatz and I.

The window in her bathroom looked out onto the backyard, but it was a section of the backyard rarely used for anything. Her room and its private bathroom had been added to the house after its construction. Compared to all the other houses which had been spawned from the same half-dozen blueprints, the tumor of an extra room looked unnatural. My parents had added it as a sort of apartment when it was speculated that an infirm aunt would come to live with us, and would appreciate her own space set slightly apart from the house. The aunt in question - a great-aunt to me who I remembered only as a sad, old woman who made vague prognostications of doom while shaking her head - had settled the matter by dying quietly rather than becoming the burden to us that she imagined she would be. We were left with a guest room which was positively luxurious by the neighborhood's standards in a house that rarely entertained even casual visitors.

All of the activity in the yard took place behind the main part of the house, and Mrs. Glatz's bathroom protruded towards woods in the back of our yard, guarded only by a small hillock and some stray cornstalks which provided an irregular curtain. Through observations which I considered worthy of a master spy, I'd discretely discovered the perfect line of sight through the gaps in the stalks from which to observe her next bath. With my newfound confidence in my clandestine skills I convinced myself that I would be invisible from my vantage point, peering over the hillock.

My decision to spy on Mrs. Glatz in the tub was not really a conscious one. Instead, it simply struck me as some sort of imperative. I knew that I was not in love with Mrs. Glatz, but she was endlessly fascinating to me. Most of the women I knew were mothers of my friends and classmates. My thoughts about them had obviously never turned sexual. Older sisters of my friends were not viable candidates for these budding attentions either, as my mind would veer off into scenarios of my friends or their parents arriving home at inopportune times. Women in town were simply too familiar to me as well. The nurse at the shaky-handed doctor's office would have been attractive to most men, but to the boys who grew up stripping to their underwear and stepping on the scale for her she would have been as alien an object for sexual feelings as our friends' mothers. Our eyes occasionally drifted to the front of her uniform, stretched tight across her ample bosom, but none of us quite understood why. As for the girls in our class, we'd looked upon them as a nuisance and continued to do so. Few of them had begun to develop, though none notably, so there was little change in them that we could see from the pigtailed targets of insults and epicenters of cooties that they'd been to us throughout our childhood.

Mrs. Glatz, however, stepped out of nowhere and delivered herself to my fragile, emerging curiosity. Any observer would find her attractive, and some would likely describe her as beautiful. More significantly for me, however, she was simply in a different category from all of the women I knew. When she ate with us at the table, she was very quiet, volunteering very little about herself. My parents had more discretion than most, and stopped questioning her on much of anything after the first few meals.

Mrs. Glatz was a different sort of breed from most women I knew, physically speaking. Her physical attributes were less an overt attractiveness than the sort of subtle, haunting details that a person could spend forever studying. The women I'd watched on screen were generally blonde and fair with a uniformly hourglass figure with the occasional brunette or redhead providing the illusion of variety, of course. On the whole, though, one was pretty much the same as another. In town, the women tended to have a series of prototypes that they had been molded into with varying degrees of success. Mrs. Glatz dressed the same as anyone else, and did not deliberately call attention to herself, but she still fell outside of the spectrum which encompassed the archetypes of the young wife, the single-workingwoman, the matronly middle-aged woman, the schoolmarm, the glamour-seeking belle, the genial grandmother, or the crone. More than just her newness set her apart; she seemed incongruent, as though a renaissance sculpture had been placed in the desert.

She was buxom and gave off a feeling of fullness. One would not really construe her body type as being fat, but she'd probably spent most of her youth as a chunky kid. The body she'd been left with after she had stopped growing was in the lower reaches of average height with a charming curviness. Her breasts were, to my young eyes, a wonder of nature. Were I to look at them with a greater range of experience, I might well have conceded that they were larger than average, but smaller than the epic scale on which I remember them. I was fascinated, however, by the manner in which she expertly navigated around our table at mealtimes, forever contorting in tiny ways to reach her arm or turn her body with an awareness of her bust that allowed her to move gracefully.

Sitting at the table with Mrs. Glatz was an experience. All of her movements were very deft. Within minutes she'd mastered our table's layout and was able to pass and receive dishes without the risk of knocking anything over or even extending a reach which appeared awkward. She seemed to be incredibly aware of space, and I wondered on the day when I watched her standing in the field if she felt freer than she did in the confines of our house or if she felt enclosed by the inevitable march of progress on the open spaces in the world.

Mrs. Glatz's hair was short. It seemed unusual to me for women her age to have short hair. Also, it was not the playful bob that some women were able to pull off, but an aggressively clipped configuration. If I had not been grounded in the idea that haircuts were a deliberate and measured action undertaken at a barbershop or beauty salon, I might have guessed that she'd simply taken a scissor to her hair and cut it off in response to some dark urge. The color of her hair was as dark and uniform as the feathers of a crow and appeared impossibly perfect. Perhaps my older self faced with a young Mrs. Glatz would assume that she had her hair colored. Perhaps I'd be able to see with certainty that it occurred naturally. Either way, to a boy on the cusp of his teens, it shone with an inscrutable dark glow.

What was more impressive than any single physical attribute was the totality of her. Whereas I was in the process of growing into my body in ways that I could not yet understand, most adults had become accustomed to who they were, physically speaking, and acted accordingly. They moved slowly and cautiously as though advertising vulnerabilities. Mrs. Glatz, however, did not seem to be constrained by her body. When she walked, I would believe that if she wished to she could walk across the entire state at speeds into which I couldn't even coax my bicycle. When she stood still, as she did that day in the field, I would have believed that she could root herself without moving for a hundred years. Part of me imagined that she could have suddenly jumped over the house if she'd so desired.

The eyes of Mrs. Glatz were a shade darker than the tranquil sky of the summer days she spent in our home. They were never unfocused, from what I could see. Even staring off into space was an exercise in concentration for them. Whenever they found me, I imagined that they were seeing something deeper within me, the something that kept me awake all night and dreaming of other places. And when they looked away, I was left haunted by that color I could find nowhere else in this world, as though they were still watching me although their owner had left the room.

The air she carried herself in was intriguingly morose. To a boy whose sex drive was just kicking in but who hadn't abandoned childhood's morbid curiosity, there was nothing more ensorcelling than having the two combined in one woman. My feelings for her were born of fascination, not any sort of camaraderie. Mrs. Glatz inadvertently enhanced her mystery by being very reserved in her speech and activities. She fit in quite well in our household, and tended to treat me in the same manner that my parents did.

Not that she was a very active part of our household. For the most part she joined us only for meals, and those were undertaken with no more conversation than we'd already gotten used to, which was very little. Since we had no television, the living room – rather than being a gathering point for sundry family members – was largely unused. My parents tended to either read the paper or listen to the radio at night in the sitting room upstairs next to their bedroom. I would occasionally join them, but it was far from a nightly ritual. Mrs. Glatz joined us a few times, especially when she first arrived. For the most part, however, she kept to herself.

My parents were genteelly ambivalent to Mrs. Glatz. They treated her kindly, but not especially warmly; hardly a surprise in light of their attitude toward me. She was given complete freedom and significantly less attention than most of the other households in town would have thrust upon her. Other families would have organized game nights or parties to get to know her. Gathering around the radio or television would have been almost compulsory. In addition, every one of her moves would have echoed through the gossip chambers in town until elaborate speculations about her past had gelled into a single unfounded story. Each version would have some variation of course, but her name would have been forever associated with some tragic or shocking tale which bore no relation to the truth. Our quiet home was surely a more tranquil refuge from whatever actual demons plagued her.

Most of her days saw her getting up early to have breakfast with us. Then she'd wander through the town with no real agenda. I surreptitiously followed her a few times and wasn't disappointed. Not that her meanderings were terribly exciting, but they were different and therefore interesting. I would have expected her to go to main street and try familiarize herself with the stores she'd be frequenting and become friendly with the people who would be her neighbors. Instead, she would just walk around until she came to some area of town that was not yet developed. Instead of the network of blocks and the stores on main street, she sought out the woods and the fringes of our little world. Empty lots were her destination rather than the no-man's lands between the islands of life that most of the adults saw.

I saw her stop one day in the middle of a field in an empty lot and simply stand there, unmoving, for the better part of an hour. Watching her grew frustrating as time wore on, yet I did not feel ready to surrender the precious moments of afternoon I'd already put into the effort without seeing what her ultimate goal was. She just stood there in the tall grass of a plot of ground – which would hold a house years later – her head slightly raised and her eyes, as near as I could tell from my semi-concealed vantage point, closed. I crouched uncomfortably behind a bush, silently pushing her to do something, continually prolonging my stakeout for just a moment more. Every time I convinced myself that she would stand there forever – and that it wasn't worth the strain I was starting to feel in my legs or the annoyingly ticklish sensations I got when the breeze brushed the leaves of the bush across my face – I was all the more determined not to abandon my post. After what seemed like an eternity of trying to study the horizon through her eyelids, she opened her eyes and started walking again as though she'd paused for no longer than a few seconds to straighten her skirt.

Other times she would venture off into the woods and spend hours touching the bark of random trees, placing her hand on a trunk or branch for a long period of time as though trying to understand some silent message. I did see her sit on a bench in the park and people-watch a couple of times, but it seemed to either bore or depress her. Just as she preferred the privacy of wooded expanses to the enclosed world that window curtains would have offered while she was in the tub, she tended, while wandering, to favor the places where the hands of man had made no – or few – alterations. These were also popular hangouts for the town's boys, but she tended to keep on walking when she found a place that my contemporaries had claimed for baseball or impromptu war games.

A perpetual stranger with eternal sadness worn like a scar, she was stuck in a melancholy limbo. I had no fantasies of getting to know Mrs. Glatz any better than I did, but I burned with the desire to see her without her clothes on. My irresistible quest for a more solid focus for my libidinal energies than the vague, clothed contours of the women in movies and magazines grew to the point of obsession. A plan to make it happen was begging to be born.

If I could have found a way to watch her as she slept, I think I would have done so. Her tub was more accessible than her bed, however, and I had a certainty of when the tub was filled, but no idea of when she would go to sleep. It would have been amazing, I thought, to see her asleep when I was used to seeing her in such a state of awareness all the time. Of course, I did want to see the entirety of her body rather than a pile of blankets and nightgown. In addition, Mrs. Glatz, like myself, probably slept very little. Sleep was a private matter in our house, as were most things.

When the pipes spoke through my wall that night I found my way outside and, in what I imagined to be a stealthy manner, went to the corn stalks. Enough time had elapsed that Mrs. Glatz was already in the tub, turned away from me, reading as she soaked. My eyes had free reign to explore her body. The water lapped gently against her lightly tanned skin. Her breasts, which seemed so formidably rigid as she sat at the dinner table, now lay smeared outward and buoyed up by the bathwater. Her nipples were larger and darker than I had imagined. I enjoyed the way her skin almost glistened in the dying light of day and the single bulb of the bathroom in turn as she shifted slightly in the tub. Her dark pubic hair stood out as a lopsided counterpoint to the hair on her head as the only two places on her body not purely and aggressively fleshy. She lowered herself downward into the water which climbed higher for a moment and receded as her head reappeared with her short, slicked hair hugging it tightly. My plan had worked.

For some reason, however, it felt as though the whole evening would not be complete until I saw those sky-blue eyes. I had always quietly rejoiced every time they connected with mine. I wanted to read something in them, but they always seemed to silently speak of things beyond my understanding. I thought that I could find out the secrets of life by looking into Mrs. Glatz's eyes, but not even time has revealed them to me. No matter how much time has passed, however, I have remained convinced of Mrs. Glatz's privileged knowledge of the ineffable. Like a book in a foreign language, answers were present but inaccessible.

When her eyes did turn in my direction, they fell directly onto mine without any searching. Even if she had been somehow alerted to my presence through some stray noise or a sense of unease, it would have required a minute of glancing around until she found the transgressing gaze. Instead, she locked into my eyes as though she was turning to a picture on the wall whose presence and location was never in doubt. The vegetation wreathing my face was revealed as a pathetic camouflage, and I was suddenly aware of our proximity, immediately reminded that only a couple of feet of slightly steamy air and the length of her body stood between our eyes at all. As long as she met my hiding place with anything more than a passing glance, she would have been aware she was being watched; her gaze was as focused as a spotlight.

Oddly, throughout all of my planning and coordinating - choosing the time, the condition of the night, the viewing position - I had never considered the possibility of getting caught. Her eyes were surprisingly free of judgment, embarrassment, or even surprise. I, on the other hand, could feel every inch of my own skin, and the contact, which until that point my mind had shifted into invisible sensory background, of cloth and night air upon it. My lungs were contracting slightly but palpably, and I was aware of the cyclical coursing of my own blood throughout my body. I realized that she must have known that I was there for quite some time, but had neither curtailed her bath nor shut the blinds.

We stared at each other for a long time without either of us moving. I had considered the scenario of observing her, having some sort of sexual revelation, and sneaking off unseen to be the most desirable – and, in fact, only – possibility. In that moment, I was forced to speculate about when I'd have to skulk or run away to sit in my room and wait for my father to come in and have a conversation with me about the gravity of what I'd done. I could see the totality of the life to which I had now consigned myself. Mrs. Glatz would inevitably move out, and the entire town would know why. My existence in this place would become nothing other than this moment. Forced to carry the moniker of Peeping Tom throughout the rest of my childhood, I would leave town after high school and never look back. My parents, already distant, were to retreat away further from my life to become occasional voices on the phone. Odd jobs and aimless wandering through a country that was entirely different from the one of my childhood came crashing into my mind's eye. The man I would become was content and successful, but groundless, perhaps carrying the same sadness as Mrs. Glatz herself. After allowing this vision to wash over me, I gently implored Mrs. Glatz's eyes with a subtle plea for mercy. Her expression did not change at all.

Without hesitation or haste, Mrs. Glatz's hand emerged from the water, steadily rising as the drops of her bath fell back into the tub. Moving with a slow determination, it came to rest on my cheek. Something should have struck me as odd at that moment when this small, casual motion inexplicably reached across several feet through the corn stalks and over the hillock, but it was all perfectly natural in that moment. The bathwater clinging to the skin of her hand had cooled in its journey through the window and was not only a palpable feeling on my cheek, but a refreshing reminder that the moment was real. Her arm had extended towards me and then I was somehow standing beside her as she gently sat up in the tub.

Her hand was joined by its mate, which found a position on my other cheek, and she drew me closer to her until her lips were gently against mine. Having only the glamorous music-backed mashing of mouths that punctuated most movies to draw upon, I was unsure of how to react and quickly fell under the tutelage of her lips and tongue. Her hands gently held mine as I slid off my shoes. Finding the button and zipper of my dungarees, her fingers slowly undid them. Without even the slightest hesitation, her hands gently pulled them down, then glided up my hairless legs and hooked into the band of my briefs. When she slid those down I was fully erect, my penis larger and more expectant than I'd ever seen it before. I was ready to remove my own shirt, but she knelt up in the tub and pulled it over my head. Taking my hands in hers, she led me into the water with her.

I was not yet a teenager and hadn't even discovered masturbation as a relief from the urges and sensations of which I was becoming increasingly aware. My first experience of any kind was this wet liaison with a haunted widow. She led me from beginning to end, her eyes locked on mine the whole time with the same expression until we climaxed together. My prepubescent grunts were somehow a squealing compliment to her eloquent moans to hit the night air together as a mellifluous duet.

Afterwards, I lay on her breast, my cheek half-submerged in the warm water, and she leaned down to gently kiss my forehead. Something had shifted inexorably in my life, and I had no idea how I could ever sit in my room at night without reliving of this moment. My late-night tirades would be tinged with a worldliness they had never had before. The cornstalks would have significance for me beyond the mere decoration they served as in our yard. My small world had delivered something profound and holy. Between dream and vision I'd discovered a carnal undercurrent churning through my life as ceaselessly as the ocean.

I picked my head up to try to meet her gaze with some silent expression of what I now felt. She looked at me with that same ineffability I had seen when she first saw me outside the window. Although she looked as though she'd break into a knowing smile any minute, there was no mirth in her face. She was as unreadable as ever, and I began to feel very uncomfortable. I lifted my head to look over the side of the tub at the book she'd been reading, a red cloth bound affair that had no hint of its contents on the cover. With my free hand, I flipped it open to a random page, but there were no words or pictures; it was completely blank. I stared back at her expression again, and I realized that it had not changed since the moment her eyes had met mine through the window.

With the shock of being awakened very suddenly, I was aware that my skin was touching clothing and air. Our eyes were locked across the length of her body, the corn, and the hillock. I was standing outside the open window, more exposed to her gaze fully clothed than she was to mine completely naked. I tried to linger in the moments I'd spent – or imagined I'd spent – in her arms rather than as the object of her sphinxlike gaze.

I don't know how my confused boyhood mind conjured up enough knowledge of the mechanics of lovemaking to shepherd itself though that phantom sexual experience. Most would say I projected my later life and sadness atop strands of childhood memory. In the decades since that night, I have looked into many pairs of eyes and tried to extrapolate knowledge from them with considerably more success that I had in reading those of Mrs. Glatz. I have ransacked the dusky memories of my childhood in search of what I have come to call truth, but I cannot remember what happened next. I stood, looking into the open window, our eyes locked in an embrace that never ended. It is entirely possible that I am standing there even now, in a place more real than mere memory.

THE NEIGHBORHOOD

GENE RACKOVITCH

Flushing, in Queens, New York, was a great place to grow up in the late thirties and early forties. In the thirties, the trolleys ran from Flushing Main Street to Jamaica; there was no road there in those days. It was a single track, one way in and one way out through forested areas to a turntable at the end of the line, where it swung around to go back to Flushing. It was an adventure of sorts for the young.

In our neighborhood, trolleys ran down 162nd street; you could hitch a ride on the back as it slowed on the corner of 45th Avenue, ride to the next corner and jump off on 46th. One thing about the trolley, no matter how deep the snow in winter it kept on going. During snowstorms the rod that connected to the electric cable above the trolley threw off sparks, much to our delight.

There was this thing we did as kids: we'd place a nail on the tracks, and a trolley rolling over fashioned an arrowhead. Those arrowheads were put on the end of bamboo staves that were used as spears, which we threw at figures on billboards on 161st Street. Most of the time they didn't stick, yet it gave us the feeling we were African natives attacking white villagers. We put a penny on the tracks to see how large it got after the trolley went over it; our Spanish doubloons. Imagination was plentiful in those days.

Then there were the haunted houses. The depression left a number of abandoned homes in our neighborhood. One was behind the icehouse on 46th Avenue. You hardly went in there unless it was night time, that's when it was scariest. It was pretty well stripped down, and walking on the torn-up floorboards became an act of heroism. With flashlight in hand there was always some treasure you could find to take home. If you stayed long enough, your own footsteps woke demons that lurked in the shadows. A quick exit was accompanied by scrapes and bruises. Another house on 46th Avenue's corner of 160th Street had a ghostly persona that kept us skirting around it. Tales of passersby seeing figures in the windows of that empty house was reason enough to avoid it.

Empty lots were our jungles. Stones found in them were fractured by smashing one on another; the contents were treasures that were not shared with family. Geodes opened gave us sparkling gems to be buried for future resurrection and admiration.

Snow came in winter and freezing temperatures crusted it to palatable ease of traversing on the way to school. Icicles the size of sabers hanging off buildings were brushed off with mittened hands, and like daggers falling, imbedded in crusted snow. Sliding on frozen creeks to school through forested lots, your progress slowed as you broke through hot air pockets formed by low temperatures below. Leaving the woods you reached a flat plane neutered of vegetation by tractors, and near the school biting winds tore into flesh because of the scarcity of trees needed to buffer the bitterness. Wind blowing into your face had it cracking from the cold, skin tight, slapping frozen ears to start circulation.

Into school and heat, ears burning, stinging needles to the tips of fingers, face rough, heat rushing into cheeks, pushing out the cold. Fingers frozen, you had to slap them on your legs to get feeling back in them. Something about those winter days; though harsh, your capacity to endure the bitterness made you smile.

Summer had its pleasures. Mostly it gave the adventurists among us opportunities to show our mettle. Until that time I had a few minor excursions into the life of the adventurer, including one night stealing lumber and a barrel of nails from a construction site for a tree fort we were building. Passing a cemetery that night we were scared to death, both from ghosts and worrying about being caught with our loot.

And one time six of us dragged a boat from the stock way up on the hill in Kissena Park down to the lake, found some pieces of wood for oars and began paddling over the lake. Who's waiting for us by the boat dock? The cops.

So Black Bart and his pirate crew put the boat in reverse, determined to outwit New York's finest: Didn't happen. Whichever direction we went the law appeared. Just couldn't figure out why we were so important to them. Anyway, surrounded, we gave up. They put us in a police car and drove us home to inform our parents of our journey. Personally I would rather have walked the plank. My old man's belt told the tale by the red welts on my ass, which remained there for approximately four days.

Making a raft and floating it in a water-filled excavation was another adventure. Polling it in the China seas was fun until it sank. Almost drowning made us a little skeptical of sea voyages.

In Kissena Park were two lakes that froze over in winter; winter festivals were held there. At one end of the larger lake was a boathouse you could go in to get warm when you near froze to death; a huge fireplace in the rear had big pine logs burning. You could buy hot toddies in big mugs there; their heat sent tingles through your frozen fingertips.

In January, a winter fest was held for our pleasure. Huge blocks of ice were cut out of the lake and castles were built out of them, local artists made sculptures out of the ice;

the whole town came to see them. Hockey teams were organized, the competition was fierce, and Olympic hopefuls participated in speed races; the winners ended up with trophies.

Other winter activities gave head to those with daring-do. Sledding down tree-lined runways and catapulting into the air gave notice that the participants were daredevils. Ambulances were in attendance to carry off the injured, broken bones were in abundance.

In summer, dances were held in a basketball court lit by huge searchlights, with music piped in through loudspeakers, Sometimes local bands were invited to play. For the voyaging males in attendance the dancing females let us know there was a possibility of contact without parental interference. A good night kiss was possible if your ability to dance pleased the partner you chose.

They drained both lakes one year, a gift to some donor to local bosses in getting them elected to state office. They put a concrete barrier around the lakes that was a bonus for a few of us entrepreneurs, as fish got trapped in a corner of the lake hollow. With boots on, we bagged the fish and went to restaurants in town to try to sell them. At a Chinese restaurant we found a buyer. After much bargaining it was settled on fifty cents for the lot of them. An ice cream cone and some candy was our reward for our industry.

In those early days, the empty lots gave us freedom from adults' prying eyes, while leaving us with a jungle of sorts to conquer. Past the Park the area was pristine; it wasn't a wood of imposing scale, but it was a great place to explore. Tree houses were built with wood purloined from building sites, and valuables were put into bags and buried to keep them out of the hands of marauders.

Bare Ass Creek was one of the surrounding area's many tributaries, but caution had to be taken when entering it. You kept your shoes on, because sadistic youths with nothing better to do threw broken bottles in. We always had to clean out that debris. On a burning hot day, what pleasure it was to take a dip; there is nothing more enticing than fresh cool water on a scorching day.

We had two icehouses in our neighborhood, one on 46th Avenue and one on 45th Avenue, right off 162nd Street. Yeah, ice houses; they sold ice at ten cents a block. Kerosene and coal were also sold there. Hardly anyone had refrigerators, and most homes were heated with kerosene stoves.

The ice man delivered blocks of ice to your house, carried in a burlap coal bag, or you picked them up yourself for a couple of pennies less. My brother and I would go to get ice after borrowing a pair of tongs to carry a block home, even for two of us it was a chore. No one bought ice in winter; food was put in corrugated tin boxes that were set in windows to keep them from going bad.

The 46th Avenue icehouse was run by Tuttie, a simple-minded, barrel-bodied man. Many kids in the neighborhood made fun of Tuttie, but I felt sorry for him. The owner was a gruff, hard-boiled Italian who everyone tried to avoid; most felt he had some sort of connection to the shady side. But hiring Tuttie gave him a connection to the Promised Land, as fostered from the old world ideology.

Then there was Rocco, who ran the icehouse on 45th Ave. He was nearly blind; the glasses he wore were so thick his eyes looked to be popping out of the frames. There was a lot of talk about Rocco. He was also thought to be connected, as a numbers runner.

Being young and uninitiated, we knew nothing about this activity; not until one day the law nailed him in the icehouse while trying to find the list of numbers Rocco carried. It was as if he'd smelled the law and before they had a chance to confiscate the list he swallowed the paper they were written on.

Rocco was also said to be a lover of sorts. It was rumored by the neighborhood chain of housewives that he spent more time than necessary in some of the homes where he dropped off ice. Then one day there was a row on 45th Ave; a husband arriving home walked in and supposedly found his old lady in a compromising position with Rocco. All that we knew about that incident was that he threw his wife out of the house, her clothes following her, but for some odd reason he took her back. Whatever happened is still just rumor, the neighborhood housewives were left to snickering in private. One thing for sure came of it: mothers warned their daughters to avoid the Icehouses.

There's a lot more that made growing up in Flushing fun for the young. If I have time, someday I'll tell ya more.

ON OFFERING

DAVID PORTEOUS

Garry McLafferty knew other kids didn't like him, and knew why; they thought him stupid because he rarely spoke if not mumbling answers to questions. They were stupid in not seeing that he was painfully shy because they mocked his looks. He knew what they saw: a too-thin face's jutting chin and deep-set beady eyes under unruly black hair. And he knew they laughed at how his mother made him dress like the kids in old TV shows. No sneakers, jeans or T-shirts for Mrs. McLafferty's boy; she had him in leather shoes, pleated slacks and crisply ironed shirts.

Father Casey, thinking Garry's clothes showed respect for the church, put the boy in charge of collection plates at Mass; the tradition-bound old priest refused to fund-raise by mail. He told Garry that being responsible for their Church's money at the age of twelve was a blessed honor, but the boy soon saw that his job also had interesting aspects.

On the priest's signal, he gave a plate each side of the aisle and shepherded both to the front, seeing which women wore their Sunday Best every week, and who rotated clothes to be superior to that. But Garry's mind was often on old Marcello Cipolla, who sat at the far end of a back pew, mostly just staring at the floor. The man didn't sing, or even say 'amen', but he'd occasionally pick up a hymnal and skim it too fast to be reading. That all puzzled Garry, as did the man's fraying suit, which indicated a poverty thought to be long-gone from their affluent suburb. Apparently not.

Mr. Cipolla showed awareness of being at Mass only when offered a plate; he'd look up to wave it away, but then returned to his grim silence. Garry accepted that with a kind smile, but every week he found a coin or two under the pew where the old Italian sat. It seemed twenty cents was all he could afford, and he'd left it there to avoid being embarrassed by offering so little to his church.

One Sunday Marcello Cipolla wasn't in his pew. The only sign of him was a card that Father Casey unpinned from the notice board and read with emotions clogging his voice...

"My poor husband's suffering with the cancer is over. Love of his Church kept him at peace to the end. He asked me to thank you if you will remember him in your prayers ... Maria Cipolla"

At every Mass since, Garry McLafferty adds twenty cents of his pocket money to each plate before leaving them at the altar and whispering: "Those are from Mister Cipolla, God. He loves you."

REUNION

TERESA TAYLOR

Rachel could picture Jean looking at herself in the magnifying mirror in the hotel bathroom they were sharing this weekend, seeing every pore, every wrinkle, every age spot and broken capillary not just huge but distorted. Jean's eyes, always big and blue, were clotted with color: blue shadow, navy mascara and liner. Her hair, luxuriant in youth, retained – with help, perhaps - its dark red tint, and displayed it in such a voluminous lacquered bubble that Rachel feared it would topple in one piece to the floor. Jean had accumulated a hundred pounds since they last saw each other four decades ago. She covered her bulk in a floral print pants suit. Rachel thought she looked like the upholstered chair in her mother's living room.

The reunion had been Jean's idea, pulling together the six classmates who'd designed and edited their college yearbook. In a fit of nostalgia brought on by paging through the book one day, she'd emailed the five of them to suggest a weekend in New York to celebrate their fortieth year "out in the world," as she put it.

Rachel couldn't remember why she'd agreed. The girls, as she still thought of them, were strangers to her now. Adele kept in sporadic contact with Rachel, Christmas cards mostly, and the occasional generic emails that catalogued her frequent vacations. All Rachel knew of Jean was that she'd married money – someone in yacht construction, she'd heard somewhere – and had plenty of it. Marge, Sue and Lynn were 40-year-old memories to her, whose names she saw every few years in the alumni newsletter but might not recognize if they sat next to her in church.

Rachel supposed curiosity had prompted her decision. Saturday's breakfast in the hotel dining room satisfied it beyond her needs. They were still the girls of forty years ago, in better or worse health – mostly worse – and as interested in world affairs as their attention to QVC allowed, which was to say, not very. Rachel felt annoyed by her intolerance, and distinctly uncharitable about conclusions she drew, based on so short a time in which to judge. But judge she did, especially after Marge objected to the size of the tip (too big) and Sue flinched, however slightly, when the Latino busboy leaned in close over her shoulder. Lynn's conversation was limited to her New Jersey grandson's favorite breakfast cereals.

They discussed the day's itinerary. Dinner and the theater were already planned, but what to do this morning? Lynn spoke first. "The hotel flyer mentions a children's program for eighteen months and up at the Metropolitan. If we go up there, I could get some ideas for Jason's next birthday."

Marge chipped in. "Pretty sure they have senior discounts, also on weekends," she said. She grew more animated. "Maybe even in the gift shop!"

Sue hesitated. "But wouldn't we have to take the subway?"

"Ya think?" Marge raised a mocking eyebrow. "Too far to *walk*!"

"But the *subway*? I don't want to ride in a dirty *subway* car! Three of us in a cab is probably just as cheap."

Lynn saw the money debate starting. "Whatever," she cut it short. "We're here to have a good time, not to clip coupons. What about the rest of you?"

Jean pushed for SOHO. She wanted to shop. "Everywhere," she said. "Even the street vendors are high end!" Rachel opted to join her. Anything, Rachel thought, just not Saturday at the Metropolitan. Adele, reassured that Jean knew her way around, said she'd come along.

Lower Broadway was crowded with vendors and shoppers. Jean led the way, eyes darting left and right, snaking through the crowds with a purpose. She lunged over a sidewalk table and snatched up a lime green leather purse. "Can you believe it? It's a Kate Spade! And the color! *Very* big this season!" She opened her purse and gave the vendor a clutch of bills, at least one of which was a $100. Rachel thought of a New York Times column she'd read about street vendors selling counterfeits of brand name merchandise, but said nothing. Jean spotted the Ralph Lauren boutique across the street. She aimed her bulk through the pedestrian traffic and landed at the entrance.

"We have *got* to go in here," she said, and Adele and Rachel followed obediently. It was quite the retail space, with a swooping hardwood slide that ran the length of the shop – a skateboarder's dream. On the perimeter of the slope were polished wooden tables where piles of lingerie rested carelessly. Jean picked up a café-au-lait chemise drenched in lace.

"It's Minerva," she said reverently. Rachel at first thought Minerva was a brand name.

"My daughter," Jean said. "She's getting married next year." Rachel flashed on images of trousseaus, gift registries, coordinated stationery, all chosen by Jean, and hated herself for her condescension. "This –" Jean held up the froth of silk "– is perfect for her. *Perfect!* And –" she surveyed the scramble of lingerie with satisfaction "– it's the only one!" She passed the chemise to Rachel to hold while she examined other options. A white silk nightshirt caught her eye. "Too boyish," she said. She dismissed pale green panties that sported more lace than thong. "Um, no."

Adele checked the price tag on a makeup case in the luggage corner and quickly put it back.

Rachel sneaked a peak at the tag on the chemise: $380. Jean reclaimed it and headed for the register, scooping up a pair of embroidered slippers, size XL, for herself along the way. "Adorable," she said, handing the clerk her credit card. Rachel noted the total, $466.98, and fought the urge to laugh.

Back in the hotel, Jean dropped her packages on the bathroom vanity while she used the toilet, then flopped across her bed on the other side of the sitting room.

"What fun," she said, "to have a roommate again!"

Rachel smiled and went into the bathroom, where she examined her face in the magnifying mirror. I'm growing boar bristles, she thought. She felt rightly served for being jealous and small-minded, and reminded herself of her mother's long-ago admonition to take the high road in all things.

Jean's slippers and a pool of café-au-lait silk lay on the vanity, partially spilled out of the Ralph Lauren bag. Rachel lifted the chemise and draped it below her face. The color flattered gray hair, she thought; there was a softness to it. She moved it closer to her lips and in a sudden motion touched her lipsticked mouth to the lace, where a small, pale smear appeared. She held it up to the light. It was just visible enough. She folded the chemise over the stain and pushed it deep into the bag.

Rachel walked back out into the sitting room where Jean still rested on the bed, the hotel brochure in hand. With sudden resolution Jean hauled her bulk to a sitting position.

"Fabulous," she said. "I'm calling to schedule a massage. But for later. Not now. I'm totally exhausted." She reached for the phone. "Shopping wears me out," she said, "but I love it. It makes me feel like a teenager."

"Me, too," said Rachel, and stretched out on the other bed.

DREAMLAND

SUSAN ROSENSTREICH

No need to check the clock. I know what time it is. Across the bay, rays of the setting sun fan out like a crown on the Sleeping Lady of Mount Tamalpais, and from the window of my study I can see San Francisco beginning to glow like a Ouija board as the city lights prick through the foggy blanket of evening. In a matter of minutes, Richie Haines and his partner Reuben will slam the front door of the Haines house across the street, sending aftershocks through the neighborhood. Plateware will tinkle, our windows, not properly shimmed since the last earthquake, will rattle. Then they will bound up the steps to our front door, as they have done for the past twenty...no, thirty years. I can't remember. Why keep track of time anyway? What difference does it make? Mr. Haines, my parents, the parents of our friends, they're all gone now, but Richie and I, and now Reuben, too, have picked up where they left off. Or is it that we just picked up the same old hopes and dreams they forgot to take with them when they left Berkeley, bound for where? Other historians get a kick out of hearing me carry on about growing up here. "Berserkly," they snicker. "That worn-out utopia! That shabby paradise for pot-smokers! All that's left from the 60's is convalescent homes for hippies." But what do historians know?

Long ago, long before I knew Richie Haines and his partner Reuben dos Santos would cross our street at 6:00 p.m. on Fridays in Berkeley and sit in our living room drinking scotch, debating known methods for distributing wealth and novel uses for natural resources, President Kennedy was shot. A week later, I turned eleven. My parents unplugged the TV set, packed up our old Willys station wagon and told us we were moving from our sleepy little town in Alabama to a land of year-round good weather and free thinking. In Berkeley, they vowed, they would join like-minded intellectuals, change the world, and raise their children to do likewise. They were wrong about changing the world. The world would change when it damn well pleased. We would have to be the change we yearned for.

That very first morning in Berkeley, my brothers, sisters and I wandered amidst the bags and boxes strewn in helter-skelter pell-mell heaps about the walkway to our new front door. Looking up our street, then down, we could see nothing but city block after block of tidy little houses, each one set off by its amoeba-shaped patch of lawn speckled here and there with a rose bush or gardenia plant or a shrub of tiny oranges. "They're kumquats, idiot," one older brother corrected an older sister when she blithely observed that the prim little bushes were nothing compared to the fragrant groves of orange trees we saw on a summer drive through Florida.

And then there were the swept-fin convertibles and curvy cars lined up on driveways and side streets like the gleaming gems of movie stars' necklaces that we would study in copies of Life magazine. Directly across the street, a tall boy in a white t-shirt was standing stock-still, staring at the lot of us, his mouth wide open, garden hose in hand pouring a river of water over a blue hot rod in his driveway. I waved. Richie Haines. He's older now, but he still stands there, his mouth wide open, when the world hands him a mystery, like it did that morning. "How many of you are there?" he called out to us as yet another two of my sisters appeared, struggling under the weight of the file cabinet they had dragged from the back of our old Willys jeep. To me, shoved outside of the circle of my older brothers and sisters gathering around Richie, peppering him with questions about his hot rod, about football, about smoking without parents knowing, it looked like someone had found the model city my younger sister and I had molded out of Play-doh, a souvenir of the country bumpkin childhood my parents had carefully wrapped and brought west with us. I went back to my job, washing off the last of Alabama on our old Willys, and watched the red mud run its short course along a flawless curb.

"I don't like all their cars, Samantha," my daddy groused at dinner that night. It was true. Beside Richie's blue hot rod, which he offered to let my brothers drive up and down the driveway if Mr. Haines and our father agreed, there was a shining line of sky-blue and sea-green vehicles standing in wait for some kindly human to fire-up their engines and roar around town. "Conspicuous consumption, that's what it is," said my father, "a disease that saps the soul of a free people." And yet, not one week later, Mr. Haines in a white shirt and tie crossed the street to our front door and I served small sandwiches to the grown-ups as they sat before a fire and sipped little glasses of whisky.

"They must look at each other and think they come from the same planet," I said to myself. After all, the three of them had grown up in the same world. When she was my age, my mother had told me, cities had been for people who worked at desks in the towers that blocked out the daylight. Country had been for people like her and my father, people who worked land. Mr. Haines would have thought that way on his water-starved farm in Oklahoma, too, I imagined, though I'd never been to Oklahoma. But the war changed everything, my parents told us.

I listened from the kitchen to Mr. Haines's story of hitchhiking from Oklahoma to the Oakland navy yards, lied about his age and parlayed knowledge of haying machines into a system for repurposing burnt-out engines. My father recounted the sad tale of leaving his daddy's farm, where they could still grow cotton in the good years, of joining the army before they could draft him, and of spending the last year of the war figuring out how to build bridges out of ropes and planks across small rivers in Italy. And then there was my mother, who quit school so she could run the house while her mama lay dying in the only room with a fireplace. But the thing was that, for the three of them, there had been an afterward. Mr. Haines had worked his way into owning a car repair shop and married Betty the waitress. My father and mother worked their way into college teaching and got married.

"Look at them," I thought to myself as I stood at the door with more sandwiches. Mr. Haines, a farmer boy who now owns a couple of garages, is sitting there clean-shaven as a preacher, in a white shirt with cuff links. My father has a beard, and my mother is wearing a skirt that falls to her ankles and sweeps up pieces of dust with its ruffle. I passed the sandwich plate around. How was it, exactly how was it that Mr. Haines with his lube jobs in a garage and my parents with their math problems in university offices, how was it that these three people who were having a glass of whisky in our house, had – all three of them – grown up washing their hands over and over so the dirt of daily chores wouldn't foul their food, and now had addresses on the same street, and were sitting there wondering about how the new interstate highway system would affect car sales?

"You'll want to think about mass transportation if the population keeps growing this way," said my father. I couldn't figure out whether he was trying to get his mind off that log cabin down south, or whether he was just talking about the new interstate system.

"Well," drawled Mr. Haines, "that's one question, for sure. But you know, Hal, it just seems to me that people always need to get up and go, always need to want something else out there. What's in front of 'em isn't what they're dreaming of." Did he miss the little farm in Oklahoma, or was it the interstate once again?

No, it wasn't the interstate system, I figured out later that evening, when my father told me Mrs. Haines was dead, had died after a car accident. She was drunk; I was never to ask Mr. Haines about her. I couldn't feature Mr. Haines, tall, skinny Mr. Haines, coming home after the funeral to raise little Richie by himself. But that's what happened, day after day. How he must have wanted happiness for his Richie.

Mr. Haines gave big parties for the whole neighborhood on Halloween. That first year, there was dancing and the grown-ups had alcohol in their punch. The kids brought trick-or-treat bags, and Mr. Haines filled them with interesting and forbidden taffies and chocolate bars and wads of bubble gum. Richie was wearing a devil's mask when he opened the door. "Trick or treat!" yelled my little sister. We followed Richie to his dad's room where arms and hoods of the neighbors' coats and jackets slumped over the edge of the bed, like discarded scarecrows. For us, Richie slid open the door to a closet against the wall to hang our jackets. "See? Plenty of room. You could just move right in." He was laughing. But we knew he meant it.

My brothers and sisters envied Richie, his cars, his being an only kid. But we hadn't been in our new house a month when Richie all but asked my parents to adopt him, fixing my brother's bike, flirting with Eileen, a senior in high school like him, asking Lizzie, one of our older sisters, if he could help her in the kitchen so he could stay for dinner. His arm jostled the clothes as he got hangers, and I saw against the dark space a ghostly bank of gowns wavering between the wall of the closet and the sudden, harsh light from the door Richie had opened. A shoe rack ran the length of the closet floor. Pair after pair of slingbacks and slippers posed neatly along the rails, as if their wearer had just slowly drifted upward, leaving behind this tidy mark of a presence now absent.

The adults had begun their dancing back in Mr. Haines's living room. It was fuddy-duddy music. Richie waved us to the back of the house, to a huge room with a ping-pong table in the middle and a television and record player against the wall. I had never seen such a display of entertainment possibilities in a house. Soon we were all clowning around, singing rock-'n-roll songs at the top of our lungs. Richie and my brothers and sisters were dancing the Madison, I put handful after handful of popcorn in my mouth, and we bobbed for apples, too. And then, suddenly, it was past my little sister's bedtime, and my parents motioned to us to get our jackets. As we stumbled down Mr. Haines's front steps, I could hear the grown-ups singing along with their dance music. "You're nobody 'til somebody loves you, so go find yourself somebody to love." My father started crooning the words to my mother. "Dream on, silly boy!" my mother laughed. "You couldn't even find somebody to make you coffee."

I thought about my mother and father, how they both dreamt of changing the world, and now that they had each other and all of us, was their dream any closer to real? What about Mr. Haines, coming home from his car repair shop to wander through the rooms of his home, looking for Mrs. Haines – for Betty? How about that prim little garden with its cluster of rose bushes and gardenia shrubs? It must have shivered sadly until Betty came around in the morning with her green hose and waved her silver filament of water at the plants, and then, after the accident, the bountiful blossoms drooped, waiting. Was it Mr. Haines or was it Richie who finally thought to bring Betty's garden back to life after she died, remembering her fantasy of color and fragrance that had protected her from the oily grime Mr. Haines brought home with him each night? Probably Mr. Haines, I decided, when my mom sent me across the street a few days later with a plate of thank-you-for-the-Halloween-party chocolate chip cookies.

Mr. Haines opened the door. Beyond it I could see the afternoon sun filling the living room where the grown-ups had danced. On a round table beside the arched passage that led to the back of the house, a large photograph caught the light. I hadn't seen it the night of the party. A woman – it had to be Betty, who else could it be? – cradled a shapeless bundle from which a tiny, hairless head emerged. Baby Richie, maybe a few days old. She had been photographed against the western light of late afternoon. Mother and child floated in the sunny glow. Betty offered the infant to viewers. "Here, take my baby," she seemed to be saying. "All I have is dreams. My baby needs a world worth wanting."

"A world worth wanting," was what I had heard one of the students at my father's teach-in call the world he was dreaming of, a world without military-industrial complexes and cold wars. I had begged my parents to take me to a teach-in. They had been talking about these things since we'd moved into our new house. In my junior high school down the street from our new house, everyone but Kathy Byers and Sally Prince had come from somewhere else. The boy next to me in algebra class had come to California from Korea when he was two. One of the girls on my volleyball team had walked out of Hungary with her parents when she was five. They all knew about the teach-ins at Cal, it was big news in the Berkeley Gazette. But I was the only person whose parents actually taught at a teach-in. "What is it like?" my new friends wanted to know.

We had walked to the campus; my parents sold our Willys to Mr. Breitbach, the plumber. My mother told me he was born in a concentration camp and I wasn't to ask questions about that when I was at the Breitbach's house, studying civics with his son who was in my grade.

At the campus, my father arranged the classroom chairs in a circle. The boys, some of them men, offered their seats to young ladies, and sat themselves cross-legged on the floor along the walls. The teachers – meaning my father and two other math teachers at the university – drew diagrams on the chalkboard and talked about the ebb and flow of men coming and going as battles flamed into wars and borders tangled into nooses.

What a wreck the world seemed to me. But not to Eileen, my oldest sister, who would graduate in June. It was November already, and she hadn't chosen a college yet. Nor, she declared, would she. She had other plans. At the showdown with my parents, she had set the whole house to shaking as she banged the table with her math book. "It's" Slam! "My" Slam! "Life!" Slam. My parents sat utterly dumbfounded, wordless. No one in our house had ever heard of not going to college. It was what my parents had planned for, dreamt of since the beginning of time, all of us knew that was why we'd moved west.

"But what kind of life will that be?" my father pleaded. "You'll be lucky to get a job as a waitress." Oh, no. Was he going to cry? Like Mr. Haines probably did when Betty died?

"What's wrong with being a waitress? Mrs. Haines waited tables." Eileen folded her arms over her chest and jutted her chin out at my mother. My mother's mouth puckered into a little "o" and my father stared at the table. This was the way they always looked in defeat. When my grade school principal in Alabama suggested I skip from third to fifth grade, I refused. I came up to the dimple on the chin of the smallest kid in that class. My parents had looked at me, looked downward, and sighed. So now they looked down and sighed as Eileen dreamt of going her own way, following a path so unlike the path chosen by her older brothers, both of them already in college, one of them aiming for medical school, another all set to study urban planning. But we all knew, you didn't argue with Eileen. She was a genius, her teachers had told my parents, and she should study physics, even though girls, my parents knew, could hardly hope to have an office of their own when they grew up. But what do parents know?

By spring, Richie was having dinner at our house almost every weeknight. It helped Mr. Haines to know that, while he was scouring the Bay Area for used cars to stock his new business, Richie was sitting at our rambunctious table having a good, hot meal, instead of whipping around town in his blue hot rod. Dinner at our house had its moments. We would sit quietly as my parents lectured us about making this better world they dreamt of. First, you needed a vision. And then, you had to have a plan, a way of getting from here to there. "Where is there?" one of my brothers asked. "What if you like the world you're in just fine? What if you like things more than thoughts?" My mother's mouth puckered to a little "o." To say you were a materialist in our house was saying you were sub-human.

For hours on Sundays, Mr. Haines and Richie moved along the line of shining cars in their driveway, and talked about the different ways of cleaning carburetors, of greasing engines. Richie would call his dad over and they would stand side by side, with their arms folded, admiring gleaming hubcaps, polished tail pipes, spotless upholstery. What were their dreams? Even more cars? I strained to hear what Mr. Haines was dreaming about when he sat with my parents in our living room, sipping his whisky, comparing the war in Vietnam to the war in Europe twenty years earlier.

"Now you see, Hal," he was saying to my father, "where I disagree with you is that the Viet Cong aren't pro-democracy. Just because it's a guerilla movement doesn't mean it's for the people."

"Well, but Steve, you just put your finger on the problem. You're damn right it's a guerilla movement, it's their country. So I ask you, what are we doing there?"

A couple of evenings later, after we had all gone to the high school to watch Richie and Eileen walk across the stage in long gowns with their diplomas rolled into magic wands, Mr. Haines rang our doorbell, pale and shaking. "He won't listen to me, Samantha," I heard him say in low tones to my mama. "You're good with words, you've got to reason with him." He sat by my mother, they huddled over the phone.

"I know you're eighteen," my mother was saying into the receiver, "I know you can join up without your dad's say-so." She wasn't reasoning, she was begging. "I'm just asking you to think of your father, think of what you mean to all of us, Richie." Everyone at the university, the boys, that is, was burning draft cards. "You don't have to go as far as that, Richie. You can go to school, like your dad wants you to, register for classes at the university." No, Richie said, that just wouldn't be right. He believed in our country. He knew all about motors, about mechanics, he had something to offer. His mind was made up. We would drive him to boot camp. There wasn't room for my younger sister and me in Mr. Haines's station wagon. We sat in the living room and watched Betty's garden as the sun went down.

The first year in our new home was over, Eileen had moved to Haight-Ashbury, Richie was in the army, my brother, too, had joined so he could go to medical school. Then it was two years, almost three, since we had moved to Berkeley.

My father wouldn't let me meet him on the campus anymore, you never knew when protesters would gather and a scuffle would break out.

That summer, I got my first job. I loved working at the library, looking at photos of Greek art with Miss Thornton, reading French poetry. I couldn't understand a thing, but I did get the idea that someone who had imagined something beautiful had then figured out how to make it real.

Walking home one afternoon, I thought I saw Richie and called "Richie, Richie." But it was Mr. Haines. Had my parents told me yet? Richie was coming home. Oh, not right away. I couldn't visit him just yet. He was at a hospital for returning servicemen. Had he been shot? I asked, wondering why my parents wouldn't have told me. No, nothing like that. But he had been wounded, that was for sure. He'd be fine, he'd be coming home in a few days; my mother was planning a nice supper for us all. He'd be fine. You just had to tell him that he wasn't flying a plane, he wasn't looking down at the fields of fleeing women and children, his feet were on the ground, even if he couldn't feel a thing.

The supper for Richie was his favorite foods: my mother's southern fried chicken, done up in corn meal and her special mix of Crisco and butter, Lizzie's buttermilk biscuits, and California food, too, including a salad of avocadoes and oranges Mr. Haines brought over.

We had cake for dessert, but Richie excused himself. "See if he won't have a slice of cake," my mother said, so I followed Richie outside, holding the plate with both hands. Richie crossed the street to the little garden. I sat on the Haines house front steps and held the plate. You couldn't see many stars, the streetlights were too bright, but Richie looked up anyway and started counting.

"Come on, Richie Haines," I teased. "You can't find enough numbers for all those lights up there."

"Sure I can." And he started making up words for numbers beyond a trillion. "Infinimillion, eternitillion. Your turn."

"Californamillion, Berkazillion, Richahillion." We laughed so hard the cake slid to the ground. We went back to the dinner at our house. My brother was playing the ukulele, Mr. Haines was singing "Aloha oi" and my mother sliced more cake for Richie.

Mr. Haines was going elk hunting out in Wyoming. Should he take Richie? No, my parents counseled. Better leave him home, away from guns, let him get used to working down at Mr. Haines's new Chevy dealership. A couple of nights later, my father talked Richie into going to a town meeting with him. There was talk of building down at the bay front, massive stores and huge parking lots. My parents were livid. Tell people all they could do was shop all day? What kind of Berkeley would that be? Fight the fat cats, my mother yelled as they left.

The next morning, my dad could barely swallow his coffee. Richie was a phenomenon, no doubt about it. Everyone had shut right up when the mayor gave him the floor. "I tell you, Samantha," he said to my mother "you could've heard a pin drop when that boy finished speaking." Richie's voice, soft now that he was home from the war, had filled that meeting hall, my daddy said. "It sounds crazy, I know," he went on, "but it was like Richie was speaking from somewhere far away." What exactly had he said? The words he had heard for years as he sat at our dinner table, my parents' talk of community, the people, our shared future, all those grand thoughts had found their way into his plan for the bay front. He called it development with a view. "It was very poetic, the way he ended up," my father said, looking first at my mother, then down at his hands.

"We need to keep that view across the bay," Richie had told his listeners, "that's Berkeley's little secret, our dream of what lies out there. What's beyond Berkeley? The fog helps, or call it smog if you want, or maybe it's just mist coming down from our hills. The thing is, it's a picture, a mysterious place we dream of, where we never stop wanting to go." Six years later, Richie started law school.

Shopping centers eventually lined the freeway along the bay front. These days, traffic congestion has gotten so bad it's really better to sit at home and imagine San Francisco. Unless you want to ride BART. But what with serving on the City Council and teaching at the university, I don't have time for all that running around. Besides, Richie plans to run for mayor in the next election, and we have to practice his debates on Friday nights. Sometimes I think I might move back to Alabama or live in Thailand for a few years. But every time I think about going somewhere else, I remind myself that my parents moved all the way to Berserkly so their kids could change the world. I'm waiting around to see if that ever happens.

THE WAIT

Jean Schweibish

"You've got to be kidding!" Dylan Jones angrily snapped. "This was supposed to go down tomorrow night, and now you tell me it's pushed back a week? *A whole fuckin' week*! What am I supposed to do - go *shopping*? This is *not* the time frame of our agreement!"

"Look," Max Maloney calmly said, "you'll be paid for the down time. We had a little glitch, and it's being worked on."

"A *glitch*. That's just great. This *glitch* means I'll have to come back here. That's a helluva plan, Max. Once, fine, but twice... Someone who works here notices me, and when this all goes down guess who's ID'd to the cops and becomes 'a person of interest'!"

Max, shifting in his seat in annoyance, said "Look, we can't do this yet, and I need a little chill put in your attitude if you want to continue working for me. If you don't think you can handle this minor delay...if you want out, Dylan, fine - but don't expect to hear from me about any jobs after this. Your choice, make it now. I'll need to make a few calls if you're bailing."

Dylan turned on his heel, got as far as the hotel room door and turned part way back. "Fuck it. Call me," he said. "I'm your guy. I'll figure out something to do with my time."

With great effort, he closed the door softly behind him. *No sense in sending further hostile signals*, he thought, as he walked down the hall towards the escalator, re-playing the conversation in his head. What the fuck did this "glitch' exactly look like? He had decided not to push for details, better he didn't know, and right now Max wasn't in such a happy mood anyway. But Dylan was sick and tired of waiting, not just with *this* job, but all the accumulated time spent cooling his heels over all the years he'd been in this line of work. It had come out in his tone of voice unexpectedly as he'd balked at the news. Max had justifiably called him on his attitude and given him an out, but he couldn't afford to walk - he needed the money. Every fiber of his body screamed for movement, for action, not this delay. He stood still at the top of the hotel escalator, blindly searching for some other option.

* * * * * * *

Genna Galbraith gathered her thoughts in anticipation of the meeting she was about to go into. With a quick shake of her head to concentrate on the now, she looked up to see where she'd be heading before stepping on the escalator. As her scan reached the top of the moving incline she saw a man standing motionless, his head tilted as though he was studying the down escalator's treads. Gathering some inner reserve, she mused; one could see it in the way he held his body. Like a diver, she thought, his stillness indicative of concentration. She couldn't see the man's features; the sunlight at that higher level of the hotel's atrium made his face an opaque blur. She vaguely wondered what his expression would reflect if she could make it out. She looked down and studied the silent progress of the black and silver treads herself. She had no idea what was about to be set in motion. She was simply anticipating the reunion with her old swim coach. She had a 'meet,' she thought, amused at the past and present connotation of the word, then looked down to be sure of her first step.

* * * * * * *

Poised in front of the down escalator, Dylan had decided that a good couple of miles spent in his running clothes would ease the internal tension that accompanied his cabin fever. He'd follow the run with a cool shower, and then dinner - a steak chased with a few cold beers. It wasn't the most complicated plan, but it would burn off some of the jitters of waiting. He abruptly realized he'd been blocking the escalator when someone tapped him on the shoulder and a man's nasal voice asked if he was "planning on getting on anytime soon?" He controlled his first impulse, which was to turn and pick the guy up bodily and toss him down the escalator. Dylan clenched his teeth to avoid even a verbal conflict and stepped out of the way, tipping up his palm and motioning it forward to make an "after you" gesture, then stepped onto the escalator right behind the jerk with the big mouth.

He was moving down now, his hands at his sides, clenching and unclenching as he stared at the guy's expensively-suited back. Not too late to just bump the guy off balance, he mused. But then something light caught the corner of his vision on the upward bound escalator and, distracted from The Suit, he shifted his eyes to the right. A tall, slender female form had just been elevated from the shadowed lower levels into the light pouring down from above. As he turned his head in the woman's direction, he saw that she was fully concentrated on him for some reason. He had a quick look at her features - long face, aquiline nose, and liquid brown eyes framed by a short, feathery haircut. The hairs on the back of his neck did their funny little warning dance, and he wondered why as he turned his head and looked back over his shoulder to watch as she rose above him. She had already turned her face forward in anticipation of reaching the uppermost floor, and all that he could see of her now was her back. She had on a simple sleeveless summer dress with a short-skirt that hovered over a nice pair of legs. He couldn't quite make out her ankles and feet from his descending angle, so he quickly scanned up again, caught well-toned arms and then, like some magic trick, the blurring opaque light at the uppermost floor crowned her blond head with a halo as she stepped off the escalator. He released the breath he hadn't realized he'd been holding, and softly said, "Now there goes the perfect distraction." He headed to the lobby to find a seat facing the escalator and began the waiting game.

SKIN

JOYCE deCORDOVA

"Hey nigger, nigger turned inside out" she yelled. And, of course, I turned my head towards the girl who said it, eight-year-old Carol Walsh. Carol was the darling of Manhattan's West 96th Street. She had blond Shirley temple curls, big round eyes and milk white skin. She wore pinafore dresses and short white socks with Mary Jane shoes. Very fashionable for a young girl in the 1940's. She was beautiful. She never got dirty. I was so glad she noticed me. I didn't care what she called me. The first time the kids on the block said it, I was hurt, but I was getting used to it and it didn't hurt so much now. I kind of thought of it as a pet name ... you know, like the one you give someone not in your league, but for whom you have a fondness ... like a slave with a master or an indentured servant with his lord.

The phrase "nigger turned inside out" had to do with the color of my skin. It was olive toned and, in summer, it was even darker. Actually, my eight-year-old brain reasoned that the description was probably correct. I thought that if you turned a "nigger" inside out, the color would be just like mine. How could I be angry or hurt about something that was true? So I smiled and went over to her and patiently waited to be told what to do.

She turned towards me, her mouth a perfect rose colored bow. She opened it and said, "Do you want to be an ender"? An ender? Me? Even though I knew I could jump rope faster and higher than any of the girls on the block, I grabbed at the chance to be part of the group. Turning the rope was better than sitting on the stoop watching them have fun. There were four girls and they were going to let me play! "Sure," I said, and grabbed one end of the rope while Mary Walsh, Carol's eleven-year-old retarded sister, was handed the other end. I turned the rope for what seemed forever. Our rules of jump rope were that when you missed a skip, you would take an end. This way, during the course of a game, everybody got a chance to jump. Even though it was a hot and muggy August day, it didn't stop those four girls from jumping their brains out.

Speaking of brains, even Mary, the retarded ender, got her chance to jump. I finally and timidly asked Carol if I could have a turn. "OK nigger," she said, and she took my end. I was so grateful. She was being fair. After all, everyone should get a turn. I quickly went to the back of the line (I knew my place!). I eased into the rope facing Carol. She pulled the rope. I missed the skip. She handed me the rope, looking to see if I would say something. I didn't. I went back to being an ender for the rest of the afternoon.

That night, after dinner, I decided to do something about my color. There was no point in rationalizing or faking indifference anymore. I needed to belong. I knew I could do nothing about being the only Italian on a block filled with Polish and Irish. But I could do something about being a *dark* skinned Italian. So I went to the bathroom, locked the door and took my grandmother's Clorox bottle and rubbed it into my skin ... all over, especially my face (I was careful around my eyes). Saying a prayer (I believed in prayer in those days), I opened my eyes and looked into the mirror, willing my color to change. It didn't, except for the angry rash I had on my face that lasted a week.

EXTREME UNCTION

KIT STORJOHANN

By the time the croaks of the crows had ridden the warm breezes, sifted through the gardens and palm trees, edged along the sandy paths cobwebbing Akko, and slipped into narrow window slits in the walls of the Hospitallers' stronghold, they'd become a rolling staccato barrage against the stone walls. Whether the scavengers had found the flesh of an unlucky Saracen or crusader to pick apart in the sands, or were simply chattering in their inimitable dialect, the subtleties of circumstance were lost to the crowsong that reached my ears. Mine was a dusky existence, lived in shadows with brief forays into the sun. The halls of fellowship and fortitude had been expanded inch by inch into tunnels that formed a second city beneath the one which stood under the sun, giving us a subterranean freedom of sorts. Still, I cherished the occasions on which I was able to walk the streets. My most treasured times were ones in which I had leave enough to stand near the sea walls and watch the waves endlessly roll in an azure testament to God's grace. In lieu of this, I settled for purposeful quasi-marches along the streets on official business, my sword and mantle providing passport through the throng. Or else I would covertly emerge into the night without the leave of my superiors.

Unmediated communion with the sky, however, was not free of vexation or dangers. We claimed the city by the grace of Christ's redemption, by the authority Holy Mother Church, and by the right of conquest. Yet the people who I was supposed to revile as enemies stayed and carried on much as they always had. Jerusalem proper, that holy city with the bones of the church fathers and the streets which had known the footsteps of our Lord, had dispensed with the possibility of insurrection, or even peaceful intercourse, by simply slaughtering all of the Saracens their initial conquest found, and leaving the rest to wander bereft in the desert or wear chains of slavery until conversion or death manumitted them. I questioned the wisdom of this even while hearing it, so brutal did it seem to me. In the intervening years, however, time and forbidden bonds of friendship with Saracens, Jews and heretics of all stripes have caused me to see such an action as absolutely inhuman. No one with whom I have broken bread has even slightly reflected the monstrous caricatures painted by our zealous priests and feared as shadowy demons by our citizens. As a chaplain and a surgeon, I am expected to serve those who languish in the halls of our hospital, offering either a second purchase of this life or counsel for those entering the next. My authority does not encompass any efforts to sway those who suffer from hate. It is just as well, since I would have no idea how to even begin to preach against their enmity.

Being the third son of a renowned but poor knight imparted me with a noble name, but no fortune or prospects. My skill in study brought me the accolades of tutors who thought that the religious life might suit me better than the military. My father was not quite amenable to shipping his son off to wander about a monastery in a habit and chant Latin to deaf stones. There was glory to be had, he felt, and the Hospitallers would be a better way to win it. I knew he dreamed of the red cross of the newer Templar order on my surcoat, his son a sword in the hands of the Church. My skill, however, was not with the sword but the scalpel. My father spoke fondly of me once the decision was made that I would enter the order of the Hospitallers - and, I imagine, told fanciful stories of my exploits in the lands of Christ. If he still lives, he can talk all he wishes of violent glory; I have known none.

I do not carry the same skill in battle that many of my brother knights do. Yet I carry much else that not even the King can make claim to. I carry the memories of the elder brother Hospitallers who trained me, who told stories of the early days of the hospital in Jerusalem, when the approach of the black mantle and its white cross heralded medicine and alms rather than a thunder of hooves and thirsty sword. I carry the friendship of peoples of all of these different paths including Muslims, Jews, the lowly and the lepers. I carry the faces of the downtrodden who search for me on the streets of Akko each day, hoping for me to sally forth from the fortress to distribute alms. I carry the knowledge of the Group that meets in secret, where everyone is free to speak of his or her own encounters with the Divine. I carry the knowledge that I saved one of the most vicious, Christian-hating Muslims in the city, leaving him convalescing in the home of his family with a *frange* to thank for his life. I carry a love of the example of Christ that I have never had cause, even now, to doubt. I carry a dagger, a gift from a wandering Tuareg who extended friendship without question and will carry the story of my life to distant sands. I carry the knowledge that my two closest friends still walk safely through this world. I carry the divinely inspired prediction of one of them that this kingdom will not last long, nor herald the hoped for return of Christ.

Brother Tancred can likely trace his ancestors back to The Garden if he wished, so expansive is his memory and so incisive the preternatural sense he enjoys. He chooses not to dwell on the past, however, save how the sojourn of our Lord and Savior in this vale of tears forever shaped it. His love of God is unquestioning and unequivocal. Whereas many of us, myself included, will occasionally ask Our Father why such a thing has been rendered this way or that, Tancred merely smiles in gratitude. He tells stories of times he cannot possibly remember, full of details he could not reasonably know, but I never doubt his word. He once told me of the last stand of the Jewish Sicarii - a favorite subject of Midyan, our young friend and member of our Group - who died at their own hands rather than bow to the Roman yoke, peppering his accounts with lists of the names, ages and personal anecdotes of the dead. I did not question how he came to know such things, for he sees what he should not be able to, and I have little doubt that it is a gift from the Almighty in recognition of his piety.

Smaller than most men, with features as dark as an Arab and hair as black as a crow's crown, he is hearty and tireless. A ghost in the libraries, he knows where every volume is located, and reads perfect Greek, Arabic, Hebrew, Frankish and various German and Italian dialects in addition, naturally, to his native English and Latin. I've heard him make strange, musically-stabbing mumbles which he said others in his isles spoke rather than his trilling and inflective cradle tongue. Sometimes he speaks from the depths of human history in words that cannot have been heard by any now living, and he does it without guile, as though spirit directs him. Mistaken sometimes for a teenaged novice when his hood is drawn up, he nevertheless answers any who greet or question him with total respect, letting his soft voice sift through the words to land with the gentle lilt of a hymn.

Brother Tancred wended into my life like a wind. The hoods of the Benedictines are usually drawn as they wander the grounds of the fortress, despite the heat. They are benign phantoms sliding along corridors on private errands. We hear their chants drifting into the air in subdued celebration of the Hours. Rarely would my path lead to the library, and if some particular case did demand further reading, I took little note of the wraithlike scribes scattered amongst desks drawn as close to the windows as possible. Their endless task of transcribing runic wisdom existed more for its own sake than for disseminating to the lettered. On one of my rare visits to the tomes - researching alleged antidotes for an invisible poison some nobleman felt was being spirited into his food by the Saracens - I felt Brother Tancred's eyes on me. I then saw his now familiar and cherished face looking up at me from his manuscript with a pleasant half-smile. He stood up and gently glided past his fellow scribes to whisper to me "You may need to study the herbarium of al-Dinawari to create some plausible explanation for the impotence which bedevils your patient. It's a bit troublesome to access, however. You would be better off to prescribe something a bit more germane to the problem he refuses to give voice to. He will create whatever explanation he wishes."

"Thank you," I stammered a bit too loudly for the sacred silence that pervaded the library.

He just smiled. A few days later, I found myself in the yard staring at the sky. My thoughts were taken by the needs of several convalescing patients and the chronic lack of supplies which forever plagued my infirmary. "Sunlight is such a blessing," said a voice from beside me. I looked at the speaker, and wondered for a moment if he was a simpleton, able to forget the myriad troubles assaulting us daily through pure dullness of wit, but I recognized him from the library and agreed out of politeness. As I reassessed the sky, however, I was able to see it anew, and realized that he was right. From that day I have considered myself blessed to have found a friend who is a constant reminder of God's love and benevolence.

Looking like a solid tower of flesh stuffed into simple black clothing, Denis's sad, blue eyes have a milky hue creeping in around the edges of his irises. I learned that although he was renowned for his hawk-like gaze in his past -

serving as an archer in crusading armies and as a lookout onboard ships, hoisting his bulk up the riggings to the topcastle as effortlessly as a spider - his eyes were slowly losing the power of sight. His spiritual vision, however, had not dimmed, and the patience he extends to his fellow man is so indiscriminate and inexhaustible that in my less lucid moments I imagined him as yet another incarnation of our Savior.

After years of battle, he had melted down his swords and armor, and donned simple peasant's clothing, wandering further into the world than I imagined possible. His travels had led him back to the seat of conflict in the Kingdom of Jerusalem where he roamed like a shadow, making a living by performing menial work wherever he could. By the time I arrived at the fortress in Akko his travels had almost completely stopped, his fingers finding delicate and bloodless work with wood a joyous coda to the strong-armed butchery with which he had tried throughout his earlier life to honor our Redeemer.

When I first noticed him, Denis was in the courtyard carving angels into decorative beams. I happened to be watching as his head rose like that of a wary bird. Some sound that escaped my ears was a veritable alarm bell to his, and he set down his tools, covered them with a cloth, and approached the gate. A moment later desperate mewling became audible. "Bloody Saracens!" I heard a man at the front gate screaming at the top of his lungs. The guards stood back to let in a young man who had blood flowing from several places. His hands were coated as though he were wearing burgundy gloves, and blood streamed down his face as rain might on the glass window in the abbot's room. Streams of his curses flowed out as he swore revenge on all Saracens, loudly planning the means of sating his newborn bloodlust, calling down vengeance in the names of the saints. Instead of watching the poor fellow lumbering in pain as others did, Denis scooped him up like a mother would a child, and carried him towards my infirmary.

"You are in good hands," he assured the man, though he did not know me from Adam. His step never faltered as he carried the battered creature into my infirmary and gently laid him down on a straw mattress. The man was thrashing about in his fury scattering straw in his paroxysm of anger. The black-clad carpenter laid his hand on the face of the man, despite the mask of blood. The victim gasped for a moment, then slowed his breathing to a normal level.

Denis held his hand and calmed him with tales of Saint Leonard of Noblac and his intercession on behalf of all prisoners while I worked to staunch the blood. He spoke of Bohemond himself owing his liberty to Saint Leonard. "It is a tale I tell myself when I feel bound by hatred, a much deeper prison than any man can devise. Saint Leonard has melted my own chains more times than I can remember. I will return later and pray to him with you. For now, please rest in the hands of the good brother."

"Thank you, Father."

"I am not a priest," the man in black smiled at him. "But you are most welcome."

By the time he had finished talking I had most of the blood cleared away and had bandaged the man as best I could. I held him up and bade him drink a tincture to bring about the slumber needed to help convalescence. By the time my patient had slipped off to sleep, the man in black was gone.

I encountered him later that day in the courtyard where he was carving grotesque, demonic figures in what was shaping up to be a pillar. "Thank you for your assistance," I said.

"Will he recover?"

"He will be sore for some time, but his wounds should heal."

"Good."

"Why did you invoke Saint Leonard?" I asked.

"The goodly saint is protection against footpads. And that is what our friend was the victim of. Whether they were Muslim or Christian, I know not. Nor does he."

"I cannot vouch that he will not seek vengeance once he is on his feet again."

"Nor can I. But I shall pray with him nonetheless. Every thief has only one religion. It would be a shame if he were to attack a Muslim for the sins of a Mammonite."

"Michel," I offered.

"Denis."

In the intervening years his eyes have faded faster and faster, but he sees the hearts of men no less clearly than he did that day.

It had become habit for me to enlist their assistance when leaving the compound for any length of time. Brother Denis, after a great number of years of traveling and learning from the world at large, had opted for the life of an oblate in Akko. His woodworking skills were more use than his instinct for battle these days. Despite his fading eyesight, he was very precise with small, delicate work. Yet his duties were not urgent enough that his bulk could not be enlisted to help project strength when I traveled about. Brother Tancred's skill in the scriptorium was much praised, but almost unnecessary in a largely military milieu. As a result, both are ready at a moment's notice to drop duties and accompany me if I have a particular task to perform. The day of the bloody encounter would see them by my side yet again as a sacred duty presented itself.

Listening to the crows that morning, I did not think much of glory, but of how the walls of the hospital would likely soon be witness to the voices of screaming men, the latest casualties from a seemingly unending stream of skirmishes. Not a day went by, even in that nominal oasis of peace, in which I was not called upon to practice my art on some unwary man. Too many days saw me exercising my office to grant extreme unction to some unfortunate soul who had been rotting to pieces from festering wounds. In theory, the Saracens stayed in their own sections of Akko and we did not wander far from our own buildings without the cover of a large company. In practice, however, robed Muslims wandered the streets as fleetingly and securely as incorporeal ghosts, despite the fact that a Christian who cut one down in the street would face little discipline or reprimand. In practice, Christians who found themselves lost in strange streets almost constantly turned up in pieces in ash heaps. In practice, I myself had seen the outside of the walls many more times than is safe for a Christian, or seemly for one of my order. In theory I was supposed to be surrounded by danger. In practice, I did not feel that I had any enemies at all.

My nocturnal activities had come under scrutiny by Master Ældbert, who chastised me for being too free of speech and too familiar with all. In our new Jerusalem, I was told, we were expected to be as unapproachable as saints. We were to lead and inspire, not to be friends and equals. "Warmth of manner is but cold comfort," he would say, "to a rotting body on the sands or a soul in the pits of Hell." My bedside presence was criticized as too soft, too engineered towards comfort to be effectual against the disease and injury we encounter. My patients, who survived in great numbers, tended to disagree. As would the secret Group of which I was a member, from whom I learned compassion, much as our Lord and Savior showed towards everyone he met, regardless of station or tribe. I made no comparison, of course, but I proudly cited His example as the path I was content to follow.

"Brother Michel," Master Ældbert began in as much patience as he could muster when I answered his summons. "I have received word of a Lady of great station who is dreadfully ill."

"Is she expected to survive?"

"Please do not probe me with questions. It is impudent."

"Apologies, Master."

Ældbert gritted his teeth, rattled off what I assumed were curses in whispered English, and sighed. "The lady seems to have given up hope. Her husband, however, who is most supportive of our efforts here, has not. I would like you to assess the situation and offer her medicine, counsel, or final absolution as the case might warrant."

"Yes, Master."

Within a half-hour I had enlisted the company of Brother Denis and Brother Tancred, and we were walking the streets, a black-clad trio on our way to either save a woman's body or soul, depending on how the Divine was willing to dispose the day. Our course was well-trodden for the most part and the villa of the lord and his ailing lady was known to us. Street after street greeted us with hushed deference in the midst of buying, selling, gossiping, or squabbling. A single diversion from a major thoroughfare to a side street, however, delivered us to a world as different as the moon.

In the middle of a dusty street of shallow alcoves carved into crumbling walls, the sounds of daily life suddenly stopped as though a door had been closed. There were no market stalls, no sailors jostling their way through crowds, and no crowds to jostle. The only sign of life lay a few yards ahead of us. Four Arab men had surrounded an old man, who lay propped against a wall. I recognized the face of one of the Arabs immediately. His elder brother, Hafiz, and younger brother,

Mueen, were friends of ours, both members of our Group. This face, however, had no promise of friendship for any of us.

Ghazi, the hostile brother whose birth had been flanked by those of our friends, wore a look of perpetual bloodlust. His venom for all things Christian was the only characteristic that he willingly showed to the world. Although his spite generally took the form of whispered insults to passing *frange*, his acts that afternoon were drawing him into far more dangerous territory. Along with three chortling cohorts, he was lobbing abuses at the older man, an indigent ex-soldier who I knew from his begging on the corners. I had tried to treat him in the street for old wounds to a foot that was rotting away. Though I saved the flesh of his foot, my attempts to allow him to walk again were unsuccessful. Wavering his way through the streets on crutches thereafter, he thought of me kindly, never offering ill will for his consignment to hobbling. A few *deniers* would always be found for his outstretched hands, and he offered prayers in return with a solemn authority on par with the pontiff. This old man was being unceremoniously kicked by Ghazi while Ghazi's friends laughed.

They had been preoccupied enough to miss our approach, and their first warning was a shout that pounced out of me before I'd decided to utter "Stop!"

Denis and Tancred instinctively flanked me as I walked towards the quartet who now regarded me incredulously. For a fleeting moment I hoped that the matter would end right there, but Ghazi's blind hatred would not allow him to back down. He tabulated the odds in his favor by a quick headcount, then smirked at us. "I am doing nothing wrong," he said mockingly in Arabic. "I merely offer this poor uncle some counsel."

"Ghazi," I said. His shock that I had understood his words quickly became rage that I knew his name. "I know your family," I continued in Arabic. "I know the teachings of the

Prophet, Peace be upon his name. Compassion is more mete than violence for this destitute man."

"Blasphemer!" he exploded. "I shall have your tongue."

His dagger was in his hand and sliced the air a foot away from my face before I even had a chance to draw my sword. My intention had not been to incite a brawl, but once the first stroke was made, his friends joined in immediately. One produced a sword of his own, marching straight at Denis while the other two balled up their fists and followed after him.

My companions did not hesitate. Within a second, Brother Denis had a knife in each hand from somewhere under his tunic. He dodged the artless chop of the man's blade, kicking him in the ribs while he was off-balance. Tancred's walking staff fell smartly onto the one unarmed man before he even saw it rise, catching the would-be brawler where shoulder and neck met. He toppled into the dust, and the other Arab gaped at his fallen friend for a second before Tancred's staff caught him in the abdomen. He tumbled backwards and then limped away. The one who had been hit in the shoulder stood up with eyes full of anger and fear, but he saw that Tancred had no interest in hitting him again and ran off after his fleeing friend.

My sword moved deftly, more gracefully than Master Ældbert would have ever given me credit for, carving out a space before me through which Ghazi dared not tread. Yet he stood just beyond the blade's reach, slicing his dagger so quickly that I heard it cut the air. Denis, in a vaguely-threatening stance, his knives at the ready, had given the sword-wielding man time to stand upright again rather than attack. The man could easily have run away, but chose instead to charge Denis. With the dexterity of a younger, smaller man, Denis sidestepped the attack and swept the Arab's legs from beneath him, sending the man tumbling into the dust, his sword landing a foot away from his grasp. When he tried to reach out for it, Denis brought one of his knives straight down through the hand of the poor fellow. He screamed as Denis pulled the blade out and placed his foot firmly on the blade of the sword pinning it to the dirt. The man sat back in shock, cradling his wounded hand.

Ghazi saw that any chance he had to land a blow was ending. Feinting a stab at my eyes, he lunged at my heart, but had to try desperately to alter his trajectory as he saw my sword hold steady. He swiped at my midsection as he passed, and my blade bit his thigh as he missed his mark. Anger rather than pain gave volume to the curse he shouted as he found himself wounded and alone in his struggle. The man who'd previously swung his blade at Denis crawled backwards, then stood up, defiant but wary. Unarmed and wounded, he clutched his hand and slowly stepped back. Although he could no longer fight, he clearly did not wish to abandon Ghazi.

Ghazi saw that his friend was on the far side of our trio now. Tancred held his staff at the ready, his gaze fixed on the wounded man. I had my blade pointed at Ghazi. Denis was still as a stone between us, his stance open, knives aimed down, but indisputably ready. Ghazi exchanged glances with his friend, spat at the ground in front of me, and ran down an alley. His friend offered no spittle but glared at us as he strode off, his sword and pride left behind.

I exhaled heavily and sheathed my sword. Denis's knives had already vanished into his tunic. His milky eyes met mine, offering silent comfort, before sliding on to Tancred, who looked as though he'd already forgotten the incident. The old beggar thanked us and offered blessings. Each of us found a few *deniers* to drop into his hand, thanking him as we gave our offerings.

"Perhaps there are safer places to enjoy an afternoon," Denis suggested gently.

The old man continued blessing us and hobbled off on his crutch, no lamer than he was before the encounter. We continued our journey in silence, leaving the abandoned sword in the dust.

BECOMING BEN GUNN

DAVID PORTEOUS

Remember a Police hunt for Ben Gunn, an escapee they said was an illegal immigrant wanted for everything from shoplifting to spying? I know the whole story, but this is all I'll tell you: he's from a planet called Howff and his real name is Navigarecon Zumonskii. It's from a job he was bred to do: Navigation and Reconnaissance Galaxinaut. Navi, as his crews knew him, was in Howff's highest rank of intelligence; on Earth he's literally incredibly amazing.

He got here by accident as he was charting planets on an Intergalactic Bubblecraft. He saw our solar system's blue planet and flew closer to see its shiny liquid areas through a ViewPane, which he now knows to call a window. He checked in his Universal Reference Tome, and would later regret not reading beyond '*the planet is no threat to civilized life*' to see '*its atmospheric pressure is perilous in light craft*'. Be that as it may, as indeed it was, seeing trees now found only in Howff's museums induced him to fly even lower to study them; his Bubblecraft imploded.

He alone survived; he'd had enough time to imagine being in a specific tree and click his fingers to rematerialize in that tree. Although sad about his crew, he applied Howffian logic to assess how to survive here. He sensed exhilarating levels of atmospheric oxygen and saw life forms, so reasoned that one species might be able to converse. He activated his wrist-fit galactic translator and an implanted aural decoder told him: "*Your Nootork Stell-Cell Voca-Tome has a language of this planet its life forms call Earth. Named for a minor area named England, it has uses elsewhere. Why is not known, nor is what use language option Urdu will be. Data end. After a beep, Nootork will effect all aural and verbal translations. Beep."*

Navi finger-click traveled through trees to observe humans and, as he looked alike enough to blend in, he did and heard one say 'money made life easy'. He stole an example - pick-pocketed a twenty-dollar bill, actually - and, using his Galaxinaut training in memorized-molecular-cloning of food - it negated having to haul supplies on spaceships - Navi covertly replicated the bill in a jacket pocket before he discretely slipped it back in its owner's pocket.

He paid for his needs with memory-cloned bills, some in my bookshop, though I was unaware of it. He had found *Treasure Island* and, empathizing with the marooned pirate, Ben Gunn, he chose to take the name. He took the book, too; walked off reading it until I yelled and he ran back, profusely rueful, to give me forty dollars. He refused to take change and kept reading about his new namesake, apparently glad that the episode ended agreeably.

Something similar occurred in another bookshop, but its owner called Police to arrest Ben. He was taken away and charged with shoplifting by Officer Liam Dolan, whose fury when Ben said that he had lifted only a book named *Catch 22* silenced Ben while he deciphered Police language.

"Speak up!" Dolan snarled. "Name?"

"Mine? Ben Gunn."

"That ya full name? No middle-uns?"

"Another name? Not to my knowledge."

After a taut silence, Dolan snapped: "Address?"

Ben had to ask: "Address what in particular?"

"Yer *home*, y'idiot! Wherezitat?"

"My home is, I regret, a long flight from here."

Dolan snapped: "So gimme yer I-D." And as Ben pondered that, he roared: "Yer identifuggincation!"

"Identity? I have no such document in this language."

"Got any money, then?"

"How many twenty-dollar notes do you want?"

"Whatzat? Wanna bribe me, do ya?"

"Bribe? Make an offer of an item of value to induce you to act dishonestly for my benefit? No."

Dolan roared: "Put yer money on the counter!"

"You need no counter. To produce your money I mentally specify the number I want." As Dolan's face turned purple, Ben reached into his jacket's pocket, clicked his fingers twice and then handed over two twenty-dollar bills.

"That's it? Ya got more?"

"If you wish." Ben made another forty dollars.

"Owmuch is in there? Geddit all out... *Now!*"

"My pocket is now empty, but if this is insufficient, I can produce more."

Dolan tore open Ben's jacket, ripping the empty pocket in the process. Ben smiled because it proved what he said, but Dolan snarled: "What's so fuggin' funny? Got more in another pocket?"

"I have no other pocket," Ben said, suddenly too alarmed by Dolan's anger to enjoy having understood him. "But I will give you more." After four finger clicks in his torn pocket he pulled out eighty dollars and handed it over.

That alarmed Dolan. "Howdafug'd ya do that? Got a secret pocket, or somethin'?"

The Officer's stunned look induced Ben to repeat his action; he realized his imprudence the instant that Dolan drew out a pistol and snarled: "Gimme that fuggin' coat to check!"

Ben squinted into the gun's barrel and clicked his fingers. Only his Howffian eyesight could see it all disassemble and fall to the floor in a nanosecond of action.

Dolan whined: "Whodahell can do that?"

"I will clarify it as best I can. I am Navigarecon Zumonskii, but here I am to be called Ben Gunn. Please note that."

"Sure," Dolan agreed dully. "But *what* are ya?"

"That is a more apt query," Ben conceded. "But you will not believe the explanation, and as you can now over-compensate the book seller, may we not end our interaction?"

Dolan mumbled: "No, wait. Lemme get this straight. Yer an illegal immigrant, givin' me this two hunnerd forty bucks, right?"

"Basically, though I dispute *illegal immigrant*, so that need not concern us."

Dolan howled: "What? Arr, Jayzuz Christ!"

A senior officer came to ask: "Problem, Liam?"

"Oh, no," Dolan said; sarcastically, Ben thought. "He steals a book, tries to bribe me, then fuggsup me gun! And, Sarge ... No Immigration I-D!" He looked warily at Ben. "Right? Got no papers hidin' in yer trick pocket?"

"No," Ben agreed, but added obligingly: "However, I could produce copies if shown some. Would that help?"

Sarge said curtly: "I'm Sergeant Somerville, and you're now busted, punk!"

"I doubt it. This person did use violence which tore my ... fuggin' coat, did you call it? But all of my skeletal frame still seems functionally stable."

Somerville hissed at Dolan: "Justified violence, I'd say." To Ben, he said: "So you're busted ... nabbed ... arrested."

"I do understand arrested." Ben informed him.

"I'm glad," Somerville said in his own sarcastic tone before he told Dolan: "Get him in a cell ... *now*!"

"Cell?" Ben queried. "A room in a monastic institution in which I can rest? I will appreciate having it."

"You can stay till hell freezes over, as far as I'm concerned. Just empty your pockets first."

"My only pocket is empty, as I told this person."

"Then *this person* will take you to your rest."

As Dolan led him away, Ben asked: "Is a cell here to now be my address in this community?"

"Forever'd be good. Now geddin' an shuddup!"

But Ben had to ask: "May I have my book?"

"To destroy the evidence before ya go to court?"

"I would never destroy a book," Ben assured him. "But, if not my book, do you lend reading material?"

"Nah! I'll be readin' to see who else wants ya."

"No books? No matter. I shall get some later."

Dolan left, mumbling: "I get all the damn hard cases."

Ben didn't know why Dolan saw it as a hard case, as he'd admitted taking the book, but he was glad to see that this society provided jobs for its dimwits. It boosted his sense of gratitude for a residence, and Ben instantly fell asleep on the hard cot.

Dolan returned to see Somerville waving Ben's money and announcing: "Every twenty's got the same serial number!"

Dolan whooped: "Forgery! We got the bastard!"

"So make sure no other precinct's got a claim on him while I show these to the Captain."

Howffian abilities let Ben hear that in his sleep. He woke, but heard no more after Somerville went upstairs, so he clicked his fingers to return to my shop. Dolan, meanwhile, could find no Ben Gunn in Police computers and, seeing it as proof he was an illegal immigrant, added it to a list of charges. When experts declared all twenty-dollar bills legal, despite the single number, Dolan went to ask how Ben got them; a chaotic manhunt began in the building.

Ben heard a ruckus on his return and was about to seek its cause when Somerville opened the door and stared at him blankly. That turned to fury as he yelled back over his shoulder: "Liam, you Celtic cretin, he's been here all along!"

"I did leave," Ben said, so Dolan's inadequacies didn't cost him his job. "But if my absence caused concern, I will advise you in advance of my future departures."

As men in blue uniforms and rumpled suits crowded in, an apparently high-ranking man in the latter told Ben: "Talk to me. I am Captain Larsen. Where did you get to? And how?"

"I popped out to a bookshop." Ben was proud of using an idiomatic verb. "I returned to read in my cell. As to *how*, I traveled as I usually do when I am not flying, which I was doing when I first arrived here from home."

"Wait...what? You fly?" Larsen asked.

"Reconnaissance missions for my government."

Larsen told the group: "There's an admission!" He asked Ben: "And which government would that be?"

"Answering that would be imprudent."

"I'd bet!" Larsen turned to the crowd and Ben had difficulty in decoding words that tumbled out as: "Did he get Mirandad? Did he call a mouthpiece? Did we call the Feds?"

After a muted chorus of "no, no and no," Larsen responded with: "Shit! Shit! And shit again!"

Ben was baffled by that apparently being an order, and by Larsen's saying: "He lifts a book. We nab him, find dud notes that test kosher. He wants to pay for the book with them. Why not? He escapes ... but comes back and says he's a spy! Do we read him his rights? No, we make it easy for him to walk away. So what are we? Fucking idiots! What are we?"

"Fucking idiots," was the chorused reply.

"I wish I'd never seen you," Larsen told Ben. "I really wish there was some way to make you disappear. It would solve all my damn problems."

"That is easily solved," Ben informed him, and with a smile he clicked his fingers.

○ ○ ○ ○ ○ ○ ○ ○ ○

After vanishing, Ben went to a nearby hotel, not ideal for a fugitive, so he checked out next day. TV News had reported the single serial number on Ben's money, but the desk clerk didn't see he had some until Ben was outside. His howl of anger hurried Ben's finger click travel to my shop, which was when this seventy-year-old woman became fully involved in Ben's life story.

I said: "Oh! Welcome back, sweetie. Funny, I didn't see you come in...old eyes must be going. But that' not your concern."

Ben went looking for familiar authors in bookracks, though I didn't know that as I asked: "What are you searching for?"

"Good writers," he replied.

"Hard to find today. Who's your favorite?"

"Kilgore Trout. He writes of life as I know it."

"Philosopher, is he? Can't say I've read him."

While Ben explained Trout as Vonnegut's alter ego, two big men entered. "Customers," I said, unaware that Ben knew them as Detectives. As I went to them, he vanished; I didn't know how then.

Returning to his Police cell was a hard choice, but it let Ben end the arduous vanishing he'd done since leaving it. He instantly regretted it; a bulky, odoriferous man was asleep on his cell's cot.

"Please explain your presence here," Ben said.

"Arrffuggovv," seemed to be the reply.

Ben shook the man, saying: "You cannot avoid me in the confines of this cell, so please awaken."

Red-lined, angry eyes opened and the man lurched to his feet, roaring: "I di'nt hear ya get in my hutch!"

"You slept," Ben reminded him. "Sergeant Somerville gave me this *hutch*, and Captain Larsen did not object to my being in it, but I must admit he did finally express a desire for my absence."

"Whaddaya on about?" The hulk growled, confusion now matching his frenzied rage.

"I am telling you that this is my cell. If you wish to express a contrary opinion, I would appreciate civility. That should begin with introductions. I am Ben Gunn."

"An I'm rippin' yer head off!" He lunged at Ben, but found himself choking the cell door until he saw Ben near the cot and ran there, only to then see Ben was back at the door. Now stunned, he mumbled: "Fast little bastard, ain't ya?"

"I can be a fast bastard," Ben said, glad to have a vulgarism to aid communications. "So stop trying to hurt me and let us talk."

The man's next lunge again hit the door as Ben appeared in the adjacent cell; he then wailed of a need to "geddorf dabooze". Ben returned to the now pitiable hulk, who shut his eyes to chant: "If I can't see ya, ya can't be here. If I can't see ya, ya can't be..."

"We can satisfy both our needs," Ben interjected gently. "If you sleep in that cell and I reclaim my own."

A red eye peeked at Ben as the big man mused: "If ya ain't here, I shouldn't hear ya, an what I hear's no help. I can't go there, coz I'm locked in here. But yer not in here, so ya can go in there, an not be there too."

"That concept confuses me," Ben admitted. "But it seems to entail relinquishing my cell, which I reject. As for being locked in here, I assure you that need not be. But first, back to introductions. What is your name?"

"Bert. Albert," the quavering voice replied.

"Well, Bertalbert, may I effect my suggestion?"

Taking silence as assent, Ben held Bert's arm, clicked his fingers and both rematerialized in the next cell. Another click left Bert alone, whining promises to some deity that he would "never touch annuver drop".

Vanishing and rematerializing required quark realignment that is debilitating if done frequently; Ben needed to rest. But with Bert's loud groans thwarting that, he chose to risk overloading his quark network by leaving to revisit my shop.

Just as his finger click took him to me, Sergeant Somerville stormed in, yelling: "Shut up Bert or I'll..." A minute passed before he could add: "How the hell did you get in *there*?"

Bert wailed: "Sarge! Aw, geez, am I glad ta see ya! I think I'm in the horrors real bad! Real, real bad!"

"*You* are?" Somerville queried. "Seeing you in *that* cell has me thinking *I'm* the one with the D-Ts!"

Bert raved of a fast little bastard darting about his cell, but not really in it, so Somerville asked: "Did he look like a guy in the other cell who's not there now?" As Bert shrugged and could offer only the name Ben Gunn, Somerville wailed: "Jesus, Bertie, I was really hoping you wouldn't say that."

"Ya believe me, don't ya? I ain't makin' it up ... I don't think."

Somerville said he believed every incredible word and told Bert to block it all out with sleep. Bert fell back on the cot, but his eyes stayed wide open as he asked: "But whaddif I see him wiv me eyes shut, Sarge?"

"Open them. If you can still see him, call me."

"Orright, but you come quick. He's a bad bastard."

"Seems so," the Sergeant muttered as he left.

Ben would later see news reports of Police investigating his disappearance and the hunt for him extending to members of The Magicians' Guild. By then, though, he had a sanctuary.

On his return to my shop he heard groans and found me in agony at the foot of stairs up to my apartment. "Fell," I said feebly. "Coming back from the bathroom I... Please call an ambulance."

I now know why he didn't; he'd seen on TV that Police and ambulances often arrive together and his quark core was too frail for him to vanish. He would have instantly healed me, but as doing it would reveal he wasn't human, Ben feared that I would fear him.

"Please phone. I think I've broken something."

He suppressed his own concerns to say: "I can better heal you than medical practitioners here, but you must trust me, and I you. What I do must stay secret."

"Do it, sweetie," I said, but the agony from speaking then made me pass out.

Ben was too anguished to realize that I had again asked for an ambulance, but he understood my plight. He gently ran a hand over me, identifying breaks in my ribs, hands and legs, and he was examining cuts and bruises on my left arm as I stirred. He smiled reassuringly and, he later told me, opted to ease me into all I was about to witness by starting on minor wounds.

"I need your nose-rag," he said, and pulled a hanky from where I tuck them up my sleeve.

I couldn't believe that he'd waste time on magic tricks, but after he put it on my arm and clicked his fingers, he took it off to reveal completely healed skin. I watched in awe as he cured each cut and bruise that way, and I had to say: "It's a real miracle! What a shame you can't fix whatever's broken as easily."

"Same method, just much slower," he told me. "But I regret having to recoup my energy before I can do that for you. More so, I regret that the delay prolongs your pain."

I forced a smile to say: "An ambulance could've been here by now. Not too late to call... Is it sweetie?"

That provoked Ben to continue; he softly pressed on each broken rib, clicked his fingers and then held the stairs' banister. As he did, I could see his energy ebbing while I felt my relief growing, so I said: "Another miracle! I can breathe again!"

"Yes, but please remain still. I repaired broken ribs so they do not pierce a lung, but I must rest before I use more energy on other bones. I am sorry for the delay."

"Fixed *broken* ribs?" I queried incredulously. "How?"

"It is complex, but your damage and my exhaustion negate movement, so I will explain. But I must ask you to never tell what you see. Only then can I trust you to know. Do you agree?"

"Of course. Who'd believe this fix for broken ribs?"

"Thank you. But before I reveal my unearthly skill, I must know to whom I am doing it. I call myself Ben Gunn. You are?"

"Ellen Brettelle. Ellie, to friends."

Ben told me of the spaceship on which he was Navigation and Reconnaissance Officer and of escaping to a tree as it crashed. When he talked about now being too far from Howff to be rescued, my tears welled up. In case he thought my pain was acute while he was too weak to continue healing me, I said: "I'm just sad, sweetie. If all you say is true...and I believe it after all I've seen...you've lost your family and they've lost you. Are you married?"

"On Howff, we bond with those who make us feel content. In my reading of Earth marriages, contentment is not given high priority. But... No, I am not bonded."

I smiled, perhaps wryly. "We value contentment too late in life. If we went looking for it, we might find successful marriages."

Ben agreed and, with our rapport evolving, continued with his story. He was relieved by my showing no fear as he admitted to being the object of the Police hunt in TV news. What stirred up my emotions was when he showed concern about not finding lodgings where he would be safe from persecution.

I told him: "Live with me! I get so few visitors it'll be safe. And a way to repay you." I blushed. "But I'm being selfish, sweetie. I'll get to enjoy your company, but also have you to fix me if I fall."

He smiled. "I thank you for offering not only a home, but also opportunities to assist you. You are so generous that I believe living with you will make me content."

He returned to mending my bones with finger clicks while explaining the technique, including: "Because faults in quarks and molecular structures do not disappear, I must absorb damage into my body for dispersal in inanimate objects."

"Sorry, but... Where did my broken bones go?"

"Not the bones, only mutated molecules of breaks in them. I transferred the molecules to the stairs' balustrade. Wood, being dense, feels no pain and is not even weakened by the process."

"So... You had my broken ribs in you before you put...their molecules in the wood? All my pain too?"

"Yes. It is why I must rest, regrettably prolonging this. I am just glad you have no tumors to remove. That is far harder on me."

"What? You can get rid of cancer? How?"

"The same way, but it takes more concentration and is very tiring. Teams do it in relays on Howff. But now, as your repairs are done, may I accept your offered home? My need to rest is frantic."

I nodded as I stood up, and although Ben had told me I'd be pain-free, I felt livelier than I had in years. Smiling about that, I helped him up the stairs into my apartment, with its old lady decor. Ben has since told me he sensed calm harmony in it as we went to my room and he sprawled on the bed, falling instantly asleep.

I sat by him, considering all I had learned and recalling his gentle, caring manner and healing touch. I remember thinking it, but must have also mused aloud: "Such a sweet man! I wish I were young again. I'd give him contentment. I'd content his brains out!"

"I shall regress your age after I am fully rested," Ben said softly from his sleep.

A Hat Of Her Own

A Tale of the 70s

Teresa Taylor

What is it about baseball hats? For me it's trouble, especially when my wife wears one. I mean, it's fine on Joe Torre, okay on teenage boys, absolutely perfect on fishermen, even kind of cute on Goldie Hawn, like when her blond ponytail sticks out the vent in the back. But on my wife? I don't think so.

When the kids were little, she wouldn't have thought of such a thing. And she wouldn't have dreamed of wearing one to her job at the bank. No way. It was nice little housedresses and maybe matching sweatsuits at home, pleated skirts and blazers at work. Well, maybe the last few years the skirts were a bit shorter than I expected, and then she started putting together these weird outfits with boots and long printed skirts, vests, hand-painted tops. Funky, I thought, but I guess nobody at work complained, 'cause she kept wearing them.

And then she started wearing this baseball hat.

It began in my own home, out in the front yard. First time I came home to see her up on my riding mower, wearing this hat, I nearly drove over the driveway lights. She shrugged it off, pretending my reaction had to do with the mower.

"If you can run this thing, I guess I can. Especially now I've got time to help you out since I cut back on my hours at the bank." She smiled winningly.

That was recent news too. Oh, sure, we'd talked about it a couple of years ago. It was our plan for the future when retirement would be around the corner. She would take time off, I would drop back to part time, we'd get season tickets for the Mets. It was that vision of tomorrow that's fun to talk about but doesn't always happen the way you think.

Then one day I come home early to find her weeding the flowerbed. "The future is here." She smiled that brilliant smile. "I'm not working Tuesdays anymore. Or Wednesday mornings." And she readjusted hair that spilled from one side of the baseball hat.

It was a pretty ordinary one, black with a red and silver star on it. She got it after she played a part in this local theater, where she was some crazy wild woman witch in a chorus line with a bunch of other middle-aged women. Banshees, I think they were. I don't remember exactly. I was in a state of shock after seeing her prance about in black tights and high boots with her hair standing out like a lion's mane and her face made up like one of those women on the street. You know what I mean. I was plain embarrassed that some of my neighbors saw the show, but she seemed proud of the hat she got for being in it. When she asked how I liked her performance, I was watching football. I stalled for time, told her I'd talk to her at halftime, but by then the Dallas Cowgirls had most of my attention, so I just said something about how all her practice paid off, or whatever. I admit I was a little ashamed for not giving her my full attention, but she smiled, and seemed satisfied with that.

Anyway, it was around that time I saw her talking in the driveway to this guy who got out of a landscaper's truck. She was wearing the hat. When I questioned her later, she said we really should get rid of the dying pines at the edge of the property and I said I'd been planning to get to it and she said no problem, it's taken care of, and for only three hundred and fifty dollars.

I was stunned. There were *some* decisions, like what color towels to buy and when to fertilize the roses, and then there were *other* decisions, like where to go on vacation and what property improvements to make that involved spending more than a hundred bucks. This was an *other*.

"Oh, sweetie," she said with that little smile. "I know as well as you do which trees have to go, and I know where the checkbook is to pay for it." She reached up to push a stray hair under the hat, and then patted me gently on the cheek. "What's the problem?"

I looked pointedly at her hat. "That silly baseball hat is the problem," I said, and stomped off to watch a little pre-dinner TV. She didn't let me stay mad for long. She never did, not from the first day we were married. It was one of the things I liked about her. But I felt like I was losing battle after battle in a war that had not even been declared.

Came the day she wore the baseball hat in the house. At the kitchen table, mind you. She'd been out back where the pines used to be, walking back and forth with a tape measure and scribbling on a pad. I know I'm repeating myself, but she was wearing her hat, of course. She came in and sat down with a ruler, a pencil and a calculator and, try as I might to look uninterested, I kept drifting from the Mets game into the kitchen to see what she was doing.

First trip, I leaned into the fridge, poking through apples in the fruit drawer. "We have any Macs?" I asked.

She pushed an unruly curl back under the cap. "Just what's there. I think I cut one up for lunch yesterday. But there should be some other kind..." Her voice trailed off as she drew another line and calculated another sum. I closed the refrigerator door a little harder than necessary and left the room. She never looked up.

Next trip, I wandered back into the pantry and moved a few cans around on the shelves. "Hon, we have any honey-roasted peanuts? ...Hon?"

"Beats me," she said. "Put them on the shopping list and – Hey! Maybe you could go to the store for me later." She smiled sweetly. "We need a couple other things, but I can't stop this now."

That was my opening. "What are you doing, anyhow?"

"Drawing a plan for my little house. *The Escape Hatch*, I call it. I figure I can use a place where I won't be in your way when you watch TV. You know, just a space of my own."

"Wife." I said it just like that, to remind her who she was. "Wife, what are you talking about? What kind of space do you need? And what about the money?"

"Something small," she said. "Not expensive. I saved for it." She smiled modestly. "A room and a tiny bathroom. I want to read. Write. Rehearse my next part. Oh, did I tell you? I'm in another play soon, a drama this time, so I need a quiet place to practice with other cast members." She made it seem so - so normal. She gestured to the papers in front of her. "I'm almost done with the plans. I've got to meet the builder today to go over his specs."

Specs. I didn't know she knew a word like 'specs.' People with baseball hats talk about specs. Like the builder who followed her across the yard like a retriever loping along behind a kid with a tennis ball, coming up on her left, and then on her right, gesturing, smiling, looking into her face. I swear I think he wagged his tail.

Soon she was in the middle of her project. She'd come in wearing her hat, sawdust on her jeans, dirt on her work boots. (When in the name of history had she gotten those boots?) I'm not going to tell you she built the place herself. That would be a bit much to swallow. But she supervised every swing of the hammer, chose every window frame, even slapped up some insulation with the builder. Harry, his name was. 'Harry this, Harry that' I had to listen to, and watch him looking down into her face with a huge beaming smile of approval until I thought I was watching a play. This couldn't be the woman I married.

But she was sweet as pie to me, brought me her drawings to look at when I wouldn't leave the TV to go look outside, and when the day of completion arrived, she pulled me by the hand, half laughing, to see her 'escape hatch.'

"More like a booby hatch," I muttered, but I was impressed. The proportions were neat, the built-in storage space was efficient, the heater well placed, the wrap-around loft clever. Damn clever, the whole tiny place, and no bigger than a small garage.

"I wanted you to see," she said, "where I'll be spending a lot of time. I've still got a bunch of things to do in here. And when it's all done, maybe you can visit me. I'll invite you," she said brightly.

"VISIT you? You'll INVITE me?" I was screaming in my head, but I could barely speak.

"Sure," she said. "I mean, it's not as if we won't still live together in our house. You'll have the TV and all." She looked me straight in the eye, the way she used to when we were first married and she had a special message to get across. "And me. It's just that sometimes I'll be out here and I'll have friends over. But I'll still be cooking for us - you and me, I mean - and all..." She grinned up at me from under that ridiculous hat. "I'd like it if you could do the shopping once in a while."

Suddenly I wanted very much to visit her, to be invited to her little house, to watch her practice for her next role, keep her company while she studied her script. This wasn't the woman I married, all right. This one acted in local theater, designed her own hide-a-way, flirted with the builder, but cooked for *me*. *This* one wore a baseball hat.

ENCOUNTER AT MCDONALDS IN WALTERBORO, NORTH CAROLINA

GENE RACKOVITCH

I sat sipping my tea at McDonalds in Walterboro, North Carolina. It being late in the morning, the breakfast menu was replaced by the lunch fare, but I asked the attendant if he had any breakfasts left. He said, "Yes" and I was pleased,

"Gravy biscuit, please," I told him.

McDonalds has creamed beef on a biscuit that I can't resist. That's how I ended up there in the first place; it came close to the shit on a shingle I fell in love with in the Marines. Don't tell anyone, it's a sin to talk about chow in the service being good; you can be expelled from the fraternity of masculinity if it be known that you favored such a delicacy.

Once you leave the Carolinas, past the Mason Dixon line, there are no more biscuits and gravy, so getting it then was important. I salivated while cutting and mashing up the delicacy. The place was near empty, I had time to kill before seeing my next customer in Richmond Virginia.

"You from New York?" she said, pointing to my car in the parking lot.

I looked up and this gray-haired portly woman stood in front of me; she seemed about fifty years old. I was taken aback and tried to find something to say. I finally said, "Yes."

"I'm from there," she said, a big smile splitting her round, ruddy face as she acknowledged our being neighbors.

She wore a print blouse, more in the style of a floppy jacket; on its lapel was a huge Mickey Mouse pin. She had on a plain gray skirt and her feet were adorned in worn-out high top sneakers. On her head was a plaid beret of some Scottish origin, topped with a fluffy red ball. She had horn-rimmed glasses; their thick lenses made her blue eyes look like large marbles.

For a moment I thought it was going to be the end of it, but she just stood there.

Now I'm in North Carolina and Walterboro is just a one-horse town, so I'm not as surprised as I could be that this weird looking woman accosted me. I'd just been selling some jewelry to two ditzy broads who thought they were God's gift to the freakin' world. They flitted around in their Carolinian exclusion and made sure I understood that they were put on this earth to be the red hot mommas of the South. Before I left their store I knew who they were going to avoid and who would be their bedmates on the coming Saturday night.

But back to that apparition before me. She wasn't about to give up; I could see it in her face.

"I'm from upstate New York. My folks were related to Johnny Appleseed. Ya know? The guy who spread apple seeds all throughout New York. He was my cousin. I never met him, but my kin told me about him. Spread those seeds all over the place. That's why New York's the apple capital of the world."

I had to interject. "I thought Washington State was the capital of apples."

She looked at me and I could see anger in her eyes. She balled her fists. "Whoever told you that is wrong," she said. "My daddy told me about it, and he ain't never wrong."

She had a look that told me I better believe what her daddy said, or I could be in real trouble. "Okay," I said.

I went about shoveling in my gravy biscuit, feeling it would be possible for her to leave if I ignored her. Oh no.

"I'm a musician, ya know." She pursed her mouth and added, "I play the drums."

Now how'd I know she played the drums; it just had to be.

"Every once in a while we have a jam session. Kenny Rodgers sits in some times. Him and another bunch of jazz musicians get together in my house. They come in from Savannah and Charleston and we have a blast. Ya know Willy Nelson? Every once in a while he shows up, too. He's a good friend of Kenny's, never takes a bath though. I kinda miss New York, though. Nice country up there. Alla my family are up there. They take care of me down here, ya know, send me money, but I miss it though. If ya want, ya can come and sit in on a jam session. It's mostly on Saturday nights though."

At this point I became rather uncomfortable. She seemed so sincere it made me ashamed of my placing this woman in the mold of the deranged. But on looking at her in her untainted spirit, I knew I had no right to categorize this gregarious individual as loony.

"Bye," she said, and took her leave; adding another dimension to that strange interlude. I waved to her as she went out and said over my shoulder, "I'll remember you."

EDDIE'S GRANDMOTHER

TERESA TAYLOR

Eddie's grandmother lives in a big Harlem brownstone on 139th Street between Seventh and Lenox. The parlor is big and dark, with polished wood tables covered in lace and bead-hung lampshades that throw pools of light on the patterned rug.

We sit on a horsehair couch that puffs dust where I move a cushion. I sit on the edge; Ed leans back and crosses one ankle over the other knee. His grandmother, across the room in a red armchair, is the color of a rubbed walnut shell, and as wrinkled. Her skin is several shades lighter than her grandson's. Her white hair is pulled back from her face with combs. She gives me a small smile, her eyes glittering like onyx behind her glasses.

"Where are you going to school?" she asks.

"Saint Ephrain's College."

She nods approval. "All-girls' school, isn't it?"

My turn to nod.

"Get a good education there, I expect. No distractions." She turns to her grandson. "You don't cause this girl any distractions, do you, Ed?"

He sits up straighter. "No'm, we're just -" he grins at the cliché - "good friends."

"Friends," she sniffs. "Had no time for friends when I was in school...well, not *your* kind of friends. I was busy doing good works for Delta Sigma Theta. Black sorority, you know, one of the first." She transfers her gaze to the window. "Oh yes, there were some high-borns there, I can tell you. I learned plenty from them, and some of it was hard learning." She smooths her hair back behind her ear. "Thing was, I never needed Porcelana, or any of those bleaching products, you know. Had good hair, too, and some of them made me pay for that."

She fixes me with a look that requires my full attention. "It was Normal School," she says. "I learned quick about how to use my time. And I haven't wasted any since. Not like some of *these* young people. I know *you* understand what I mean."

She turns that cool, dark stare towards Eddie. "I know how you and your brothers thought you had time to play. Your momma raised you in that project, worked nights at the hospital, and the three of you were looking in every corner for a good time before she even got to the elevator. Don't know what she was thinking to leave you alone. But I guess she didn't have much choice."

Eddie starts to speak but she cuts him off. "And look how some of you wound up. Albie's already had plenty of trouble on the street, and Leslie's stuck with a brood that drains him dry. Couldn't finish his schooling, either." She shrugs. "At least he's employed." She shifts her glance to me. "Too many, too soon," she says.

She pushes herself up, moves toward the kitchen at the back of the house. "Get you some tea," she says. Eddie kisses my ear and smooths my hair. He whispers. "See? She likes you!" He gives me a thumbs-up sign. "White girl passes test."

She returns, carrying a round tin tray with three china cups and a teapot, a small bowl of sugar cubes and a pitcher of milk. She puts the tray on the lace doily covering a low table and tugs the table closer to the couch. Bending, she fixes her own cup - one sugar, a splash of milk - and places it on a table next to her chair.

She turns back to us as I reach for the teapot. "I'll do it," she says with authority. "I've learned some about how to do things like this, things the rest of my family doesn't think it needs to know." I allow her to pour my tea.

"Drink up," she directs us from her command post in the red armchair across the room. She looks at Eddie. "Your brother Leslie's dropping the children off in a few minutes. Best be done with your tea before *that* crowd shows up."

When the bell rings, the door flies open and four children tumble in, then stop, staring at us. The man who follows them is in uniform, with a post office logo on his pocket. With barely a nod to us, he addresses the old woman.

"Grandmother, I'm running late. The children know to behave. Lena will pick them up on her way home." He eyes the small group he's standing behind. "You all *know* how to do," he says flatly. He looks each child in the face. He drops a carryall on the carpet near the door. "Don't you?"

They nod like dolls lined up in the rear window of a car, their heads on springs.

"Thanks," he says to the old woman. She nods, doesn't reply.

"Later," he says to Ed. He doesn't look at me as he leaves, closing the door a bit harder than he needs to.

The children are still quiet. There are two girls just old enough to be in school, one a year or so older than the other, and a girl and boy about four, who look like twins. The three girls wear their hair in thick, ribboned braids. The boy's cornrows are wide and flat to the scalp.

"Say 'Good afternoon' to our company," Grandmother says. A quick aside to me. "They have to be told, see." Like ventriloquist dummies, their four mouths open at once. "Good afternoon," they chorus. The oldest girl looks shyly at Eddie. "Hey, Uncle Eddie."

"Hey, yourself," he says. He gestures in my direction. "This is Miranda," he says, and that seems to break the ice.

The little boy climbs on his uncle's knee and touches the pen in his shirt pocket. Eddie removes it from the pocket and lets him hold it. The girls sit with me on the couch, shifting positions so all three manage to be in contact with my body. The littlest girl strokes my arm. "I'm Dolly," she says. She looks into my face. "You have pretty eyes."

"Thank you, Dolly. So do you. And long eyelashes, too."

"But yours are blue," says Dolly.

The two older girls are on either side of me. I ask their names. Lalena and Jonelle, I'm told. They begin to do something strange with my hair, twirling it and running it through their fingers. Across my body, they whisper things I sense rather than hear. I bend my head closer and they giggle furiously at each other.

Lalena points to Jonelle. "She said," - more giggles - "you have good hair."

"That's *rude*," Dolly says.

"Is *not*," says Jonelle. "I was just *sayin'*. Look how straight." She points her finger at Dolly. "Your nappy head won't *ever* look like that."

"Will too," says Dolly. "When I get big. Maybe." Her lower lip starts to push forward.

Grandmother puts her cup down. She stares at the girls. "All three of you: *off* the couch. Get the storybooks out of your daddy's bag and play on the floor." They hesitate not a second. Jonelle gives my hair one last wistful pat and they slide off their seats. Grandmother turns her attention to the little boy who has so far sat open mouthed and wordless on Ed's knee, switching the pen from one hand to another.

"Lester, leave your uncle alone, he's got his good clothes on. Go find something, your truck or whatever, and play on the floor. Mind, don't tear up my carpet with your rough stuff."

There are several moments of quiet while the children open the bag and find their playthings. Lester begins to roll a yellow garbage truck back and forth. Abruptly, he bumps Lalena's knee. She turns from her book, half rising, as if she has been stung by a wasp. Wearing her bristling indignation like armor, she flings her book at Lester.

"How'm I s'posed to read?" she hisses.

Dolly springs to support her case. "Lester, you *always* gettin' in someone's way."

He defends himself. "I just - It was a accident."

Jonelle glares around at them. "A person can't read one word if you all—"

Grandmother places her teacup carefully on the low table next to her. The children freeze as if they're playing 'statue.'

As I brace myself for her intervention, she purposefully catches my eye from across the room. "Little savages," she says, before she turns toward them.

AGATHA

JEAN SCHWEIBISH

One day, I might forget the Latin names for my beloved friends. Heavens, I might even forget the common names! But does that mean my enjoyment of them will be any less? wondered Agatha, as she stared unseeing out the window. *"What's in a name..."* she silently began the quote.

"What?" she called to a muffled voice. "Oh, yes, I'll be right down. Hold your horses," and abruptly Agatha's musing ceased. *Damn it Doris, where are you when I need you?* she silently fumed.

There was a swarm of young women descending on her daughter Meredith's home for her granddaughter Amy's wedding shower. Agatha was expected to be a willing participant at the gathering, even though Meredith knew how much she disliked "hen parties," as Archie, Agatha's late husband, had referred to any gathering of three or more women under one roof.

Silly tradition, Agatha thought, *gifts of embarrassing and impractical black lace underwear, cookbooks the size of dictionaries, useless kitchen utensils of every sort and size, how-to manuals to keep your husband home - or was that keeping your husband's home?* Agatha wasn't sure. She wasn't even sure the gifts would be what they'd been 30 years or so ago at Meredith's wedding shower. Truthfully, she hadn't paid all that much attention at the time - her sister Doris had put the whole curious affair together, and she'd played more of a guest at the party than doting mother.

Doting hadn't been Agatha's cup of tea. In fact motherhood in general wasn't her cup of tea. Doris, who had taken care of their ailing, aged parents and never married, had stepped up when called upon and become surrogate mother to Meredith in the years that Agatha and Archie had spent traveling the world. Agatha had attended her daughter's shower against her will, deftly persuaded to do so by Doris. She should have been with her academic partner, her Archie, at a dig in the Middle East at the time, but Doris insisted she stay at home for this particular milestone in Meredith's life, and Agatha had finally agreed with the provisos that Doris handle everything, and that Agatha would leave for Cairo the following day. No one could have anticipated the freak accident that meant Agatha would never see Archie again.

Did they still make up those foolish paper plate bonnets from the gifts' bows and ribbons, tied atop the bride-to-be's head? Agatha wondered. Why had that particular image arisen? Oh, yes, it was the memory of sitting with Amy, who'd been pouring over pictures of her mother's shower when she was a pre-teen and had laughed with Agatha as she pointed out the hat shots. Agatha had more time to spend with her granddaughter than she'd ever spent with Meredith while she was growing up, and had taken time to describe ancient customs of brides-to-be. The banter had started when Agatha referred to Meredith as Amy's "mummy," as Archie, a Brit, would have called her. That set Amy off into a paroxysm of giggles, tears running down her face, about how ancient her mother was that people might refer to her as a "mummy." The conversation got sillier and slightly more offensive from there.

Unbeknown to grandmother and granddaughter, Meredith had been in the hall outside the door of the den, just about to enter but poised now to eavesdrop on their conversation. She'd grown a tiny bit jealous of their relationship, but nonetheless was pleased that Agatha willingly spent time with Amy. Meredith interpreted the phenomenon as approbation at a remove. As she'd listened, Meredith's cheeks had flushed with embarrassment. The shower had been a very happy day in her life, and their ridicule stung. She turned away and silently headed down the hall. Later, when the room was empty, she'd returned, removed the little keepsake book from its place on the shelf of family photo albums and buried it elsewhere in the house where no one would ever find it again.

Amy had undoubtedly long forgotten her innocent unkindness, but now Agatha thought about Meredith wearing that ridiculous artifact at her current age and snorted in what seemed to be amusement, but was really unkind derision of her only child. Thirty years ago she'd actually had to briefly leave the room to escape the sight of Meredith with that ridiculous paper headgear's multicolored bows jutting out and ribbons dangling down. Her daughter's face had been flushed with happiness and excitement above the fat grosgrain ribbon bow under her chin that held the plate in place, yet Agatha had feigned the need for a trip to the powder room, where her real purpose was to light a cigarette to calm a case of the giggles that she'd felt welling up. If Meredith were to appear before her today wearing such a thing, Agatha was sure she'd never make it to a bathroom; she'd wet her pants on the spot. *Well, Amy is a modern girl, and would never put up with such embarrassing nonsense.*

"Mother!" Meredith called up to Agatha. "I really need a hand in the kitchen! Amy's guests are arriving!"

Agatha looked out the guest bedroom window one last time, admiring the work she'd done over the years to create the beautiful garden beds flourishing down below. She liked what she saw. *Not bad, not bad at all*, she thought, *but if I moved the ...*

"Mother!" There was a note of stridency in Meredith's voice now. Automatically she blurted: "Don't make me come up there!"

Agatha, standing in front of the guest room's ancient dressing table raised her eyebrows at her reflection in its mirror. She'd been unconsciously fingering the string of pearls around her neck, and now she let them go and had a last look at her standard company getup of sweater set and skirt. *Haven't the tables been turned,* she thought. She recalled having said those same words when Meredith had been a sulky teenager unwilling to be paraded before company on the occasions that Agatha and Archie had been home from abroad. They'd expected their only child to gracefully appear before their varied assemblages of visitors and Meredith would grudgingly acquiesce, but always in her own time. *And now it's my turn,* thought Agatha. She pouted into the mirror, then turned and sulked her way out of the room and down the stairs.

Amy's friends were arriving *like planes at an international airport*, Agatha noted on her way by the front door to the kitchen. *One after another and from all parts of the globe, from the looks of them.* Her granddaughter was directing the incoming from the front door to the sunroom at the back of the house. *All she needs is a pair of flashlights,* thought Agatha, raising an eyebrow.

"Finally, Mother! Please set up the platter with the macaroons, while I finish setting out the cupcakes," a harried Meredith barked over her shoulder, pointing with her chin to a pink box. Then she stopped and turned to face Agatha, beaming as she said, "Amy and I really appreciate you helping out!"

"Anything for my girls, sweetheart. I'm just sorry your Aunt Doris couldn't make the trip to be part of this. Let me wash my hands and we'll get this show on the road."

Doris had run Meredith's house just as she'd run Agatha's, smoothing out all the social wrinkles that neither Agatha nor her daughter were very good at. And now here they were, together, holding a shower for Amy. *God help us*, Agatha thought.

She glanced at her hands as she turned off the sink's fancy faucet and wondered when she'd first noticed how similar they were to her father's. She could still recall his long, tapered fingers, the puckering around his knuckles when his hands were splayed out at the drafting board, the veins crisscrossing the backs of them like blue spaghetti highways under his skin...

"Mother?" Meredith's voice broke in on Agatha's reveries.

"Just finishing up," Agatha said lightly. "Still had garden soil under my nails. Couldn't see it in that dimly lit shower of yours. You don't want me handling food with topsoil under my nails do you?" She turned her head to give Meredith a peace-offering smile.

Meredith rolled her eyes and went back to setting up the tea trolley with desserts. She merely said "Hop to it grandma, you don't want to hold up Amy's shower, do you?"

"No way, Jose!" Agatha shot back, as she tied on an apron and resolutely headed to the kitchen island and the empty plate sitting next to the pink bakery box. She sighed inwardly as she lifted the lid, thinking about the bumper sticker Amy had slapped on the bumper of her car that morning: "I'd rather be gardening!" it said in a flowery script. Agatha smiled and set to work.

The tea cart was finally wheeled into the sunroom and set amidst the scents and sounds of female guests clustered in groups, twittering animatedly in their variety of vocal ranges, drinks in hand. All guests and gifts present and accounted for, the shower was well underway and seemed quite similar to what Agatha recalled of Meredith's shindig - but thankfully with no sign of the formation of a paper plate hat.

Agatha was in the room, but not of the room. She seated herself at a distance from the hubbub, near the windows that looked directly out to the backyard. She was once again studying and admiring the flowerbeds. After Archie's death, she'd stopped traveling and taken up gardening. There'd been so much time on her hands, planning and preparing beds and then planting the two acres surrounding the family home had kept her constantly busy and mentally stimulated. Agatha found herself falling into bed at night too exhausted to think of much else but sleep. It wasn't too many years later that her "hobby," as she called it, had friends and neighbors clamoring for her to design their gardens and a new phase of Agatha's life had blossomed.

Occasionally she missed her traveling days, but they'd been inextricably tied to her husband and without him she had no desire to globetrot. She'd talked to Archie every day as she worked the gardens on her property, until one day she began to transfer her attention to the denizens of whatever garden she found herself in - bird, butterfly, ant, bee, snake – it didn't matter. She'd address them under her breath just as she addressed the absent Archie. In fact she came to believe that a bit of her husband was to be found in each and every living thing and she took great comfort and strength from this belief.

The butterflies seem to be enjoying their own party, Agatha noted as she watched them flitting about amongst the delphiniums, hollyhocks, black-eyed-susans, buddleia and bee balm. She had walked amongst them earlier that morning, gathering stems to make bouquets for the milk-glass vases to be set out in the sunroom for Amy's shower, dressing the room up in a facsimile of the glory exhibited outside. *The bees are probably having a grand time too*, she thought, even though they were invisible from where she sat peering out.

We really should set up a beehive or two she mused. Agatha had been aware of the plight of the honeybee for quite some time, and was relieved to see the general public becoming better informed. That was the only way something could or would be done about it. Politicians were useless in such things. "Insensitive to anything beyond election cycles," Agatha liked to say. *Used to be "save the whales!" nowadays it's "save the bees"*. For some reason an unbidden departure from an original quote came to mind. *First they came for the whales...* She no longer saw the garden as she rummaged in her head for an acceptable extension of the lines to be added to her environmental version.

A sound pulled Agatha from her reverie, an incessant sort of buzzing. At first she squinted out the window to locate the bee or bees that might be confused by a pane of glass and were trying to fly across its impenetrable membrane. As Agatha focused her attention, she realized the sound came from inside and wondered how a bee managed its way into the sunroom, and why it would bother with all the brightly colored, fragrant offerings it's little bee heart could want outside. She wondered if it was the cut flowers, or some artificial scent worn by one of the shower guests that had captured its somehow flawed receptors, when it hit her that the bee was speaking English. *Surely bees should speak something more appropriate*, she thought in consternation.

She cocked her head, trying to fathom where the sounds were coming from. Her attention shifted from the window to the far side of the room where she first scanned Meredith's friends. The 'cougars,' as Agatha now thought of them after an eye-opening segment on *Oprah!* seemed to be concentrating on something outside their group, their bright red lipsticked mouths either closed in thin, disapproving lines, or opened to enjoy the peach champagne punch. Noticing nothing from that direction, she looked to her granddaughter's crowd and saw a tall girl with honey-colored hair, holding court in the midst of Amy's fresh-faced friends, her arms and hands moving about as though she were signing for the deaf. *How could I have confused bee-speak with her droning?* Agatha wondered. *They're not at all alike.* Looking back out the window, she silently sent a message to the bees - *Sorry!*

She turned her eyes back to study the blonde, and then the guests around her. It appeared all other conversation had faded and the girls and women were mesmerized by the wispy girl's energetic monologue. If someone in the group managed to interject a comment, the girl quickly grabbed the words like a quarterback might snatch a football and ran with them.

Blondie is quite the projector. Good lungs, probably never smoked a cigarette a day in her life, Agatha speculated. She caught a vague scent of tobacco smoke conjured up, she was sure, by her olfactory memory bank, and briefly felt the urge to head out back for a smoke, something she hadn't done in 30 or more years, and found she was again thinking about her daughter's shower.

"Mother?" Meredith was at her side, a glass of champagne punch in hand. "I think it's going really well, don't you?" she whispered in conspiratorial fashion, leaning down with the glass outstretched to Agatha. "Another punch? It came out perfectly and seems to have loosened more then one tongue!" She looked over her shoulder surveying the room, and turned back to Agatha with a smile of satisfaction on her face.

"Well," Agatha cleared her throat as she reached for the glass. "I think it loosened the tongues so completely that they've fallen out because I only hear the sound of one tongue clapping!" and she nodded in the direction of the tall, bird-like blond.

"Oh, that's Meaghan!" Meredith said enthusiastically. "She's very funny and she has so many stories, the girls are just caught up in listening!"

"Really?" said Agatha, skeptically. "It seems no one can get a word in edgewise. If you look closer, Merrie dear, you'll see forced smiles, and more then one set of glazed eyes. Punch or no punch, I don't see any other mouths in action."

Meredith became defensive as she always did when she and Agatha differed in their view of things, which of course meant that Meredith spent a good deal of her life in defense mode when dealing with her mother. "Well," she said tartly, "you should join the group, Mother. I'm sure you'll get a different perspective!" She turned her back on Agatha and strode into the gathering, head held high – the victor.

Agatha sipped her punch as she eyed her daughter's retreat thoughtfully. The way she looked at it she had a few options. She could slip out unnoticed to the backyard through the sunroom's back door, or head to the kitchen and tidy up, or she could cut Meredith some slack and move closer to the mouth that roared to hear just what was so entertaining about Blondie's chatter.

As much of a draw as the garden was, and as much of a drag that KP duty would be, Agatha's curiosity won out and she opted to accept Meredith's dare and "join the group." She would head into the middle of things to play grandmother and give Amy a big hug, smile at the guests (except for Meredith's, of course) and get closer to Meaghan to see what the big deal was. She carefully set her glass down, had a last look out the window and resolutely rose, eyeing the most direct path to her granddaughter.

Meredith's pack all moved their feet out of Agatha's way and shifted their gazes anywhere in avoidance of Agatha's icy grey stare, which gave Agatha a great deal of satisfaction. Amy's friends, seeing Agatha picking her way to the bride-to-be, seemed to move towards, lift and propel her, as if she were atop a soft mosh-pit, landing her by her granddaughter's side. Everyone clapped as she drew Amy into a hug, and over Amy's shoulder she glimpsed Meredith, mouth hung open in surprise. *That'll fix her*, Agatha smiled to herself, though to the group it appeared she was smiling in happiness for her granddaughter, and a chorus of "awwws" rose up. *Twits*, thought Agatha.

Meaghan had stopped her standup routine Agatha noted, a twinge of disappointment mingling with her satisfaction. While pleased to have shut the girl up and broken her hold on the gathered guests, she sensed that by wading into the middle of things she'd only aborted her mission. She was just considering whether to say a few words to Amy in front of what was now her audience, when a fully recharged Meaghan opened her mouth again to tell a story about her "funny old granny" and some of the tricks "she got up" to before she passed away "May she rest in peace." Agatha felt something resembling hackles rise, and her smile thinned to a narrow line of disapproval. Another guest began to share a story about <u>her</u> grandmother, but it made Meaghan amp up the volume and do her best to involve the people immediately around her, making eye contact and reaching out to pluck at one arm or another, successfully sidelining and silencing the other guest. *Here we go again,* thought Agatha. After a quick peck to Amy's cheek, Agatha began to slowly move away from her granddaughter.

Amy took no notice in her distraction and dismay over Meaghan's mouth running roughshod over her other guests. She had no idea how to contain the girl short of asking her to leave and that would not only be rude, it would also make an uncomfortable scene for everyone there. Amy was grateful to her grandmother for her timing, but the respite was brief, and now she was frantically trying to think of how to handle the situation.

Agatha meanwhile, succeeded in stepping on quite a few toes of the cougars' sandaled and manicured feet, as she edged further from the center of the gathering and back to her comfort zone at the far end of the room. A cougar whose toes were still smarting shot dagger-eyes at her back, which Agatha's sixth sense felt. She half-turned, identified the culprit and gave her the stink eye. It may not have been effective when she was 10 or 11, but at 80 she had the power to shrink Meredith's friends to pre-teen days and this woman was no exception – the cowed cougar cast her eyes hastily away.

What to do...what to do... Agatha chewed at her bottom lip. She focused suddenly on a frantic bee furiously trying to escape through the room's window. *I know the feeling,* she commiserated. Looking around for something to be of assistance, she finally took her empty punch cup and gently trapped the creature, then tilted the cup and slid an old postcard that had been sitting gathering dust on the windowsill beneath the cup, careful not to poke the bee. Quietly she opened the back door, and stepped out onto the slate step to release it into the garden. As she watched it speed off, she wondered what it must have thought about this escapade in its short bee life, then a small smile crossed her lips. The change of venue had suggested a plan.

As quietly as she had slipped outside, Agatha re-entered the sunroom. She looked about for Meredith until she found her daughter standing in a group of her friends, her back to Agatha. She stared intently at that back. As had always been the case, Agatha's eyes somehow had the power to create a physical sensation that now caused a prickle on her daughter's neck, and Meredith half turned and cast a frown in her mother's direction as Agatha subtly angled her head in a "come here" gesture. Meredith excused herself from the group and went to join Agatha, who was once more ensconced on the window seat.

She sat down next to Agatha, regarding her nervously and asked: "What, Mother?"

"Can you pry Blondie off stage and get her over here?" Agatha asked in a low, conspiratorial voice.

"Why?" Meredith responded, warily.

Agatha waved her hand dismissing the question and said "Never you mind! Can you do that for your daughter? You must realize by now that she's ruining Amy's party!"

Meredith lowered her eyes until she was staring at her sandaled feet and recent manicure, the lilac polish reprimanding her somehow.

"What am I supposed to tell her?"

"Try using your imagination for once!" Agatha snapped.

A jovial voice clearly whispered to Agatha "More flies with honey, m'dear!" She thanked Archie silently and thought for the umpteenth time, *Miss you my love, you were always my better half.* She reached out and put her hand on Meredith's cheek.

"I'm sorry for barking at you, Merrie, but that girl puts my teeth on edge. My best suggestion is to play to her ego. Paint me as a recalcitrant, lonely old lady and push her mind in my direction, suggesting she might be of great help. Can you do that?"

Meredith's head had come up when Agatha had touched her cheek. It was not often that her mother was physical with her. With Amy it seemed to come naturally, the adage about the bond being closer between grandparents and grandkids, than parents and kids certainly held true in her family.

"Yes," Meredith nodded, "I can do that." She felt that she needed to say something more, and added: "I want this to be a day for Amy to recall with fondness, not try to put out of her mind as a disaster. When you pointed out how Meaghan was hijacking the conversations, I began watching her more closely. You were right about her Mother. "

Of course I was right, you twit! Agatha thought, but said only: "Thank you for your apology, dear. Now...?"

"Oh yes, of course!" Meredith said. She leaned over and planted a quick kiss on her mother's cheek before rising to set off purposefully on her mission.

Thanks, Archie, right again. Agatha watched her daughter move through the guests until she reached Meaghan. She saw Meredith's arm snake around the girl's shoulders and saw her pull the chatterbox away from the group, talking animatedly to her. Meaghan looked up at her, an air of surprise expressed by a slight rise of her boomerang-shaped eyebrows, clearly visible across the room. The girl nodded her head, a smile appearing as she looked across the room to where Agatha sat alone.

Agatha had positioned herself to stare out the window, shoulders slumped in mock dejection, but sat at an angle so that she could peek in the direction of the guests to monitor Meredith's progress. The smile followed by the girl's active mouth was a pantomime of Meredith's success. Sure enough, they began making their way towards her, Meaghan undoubtedly regaling poor Meredith with a story about the dear departed funny old granny.

"Well, hello again, honey!" Meaghan gushed at Agatha. "Your daughter tells me you were interested in hearing more about my dear old granny! I'd be happy to tell you all about her!"

I am sure you would - and then some, Agatha wryly thought. *The things I do for family*. She shook her head ever so slightly.

"My dear girl, how very kind of you! I would very much enjoy that!"

"I'll leave you two to it," Meredith cheerfully said. She leaned towards Meaghan and continued in a lowered voice, as if her mother couldn't hear her. "Thanks Meaghan, this is a great kindness." She began to walk away, but paused to turn slightly and peer over Meaghan's back. As her eyes met her mother's, they both spontaneously nodded slightly and winked at each other. Meredith turned and went back to her knot of friends, with a small smile on her face and a strange but very pleasant feeling inside of her.

Meaghan, eager to begin, started to sit down next to Agatha, but Agatha had a different idea on how this would proceed.

"Lets go out into the gardens and I'll give you a tour while you tell me about your grandmother," she said.

"Oh," the girl said, a little taken aback. Remembering the task at hand however, she regained her self-confidence and said "Okay, that would be nice. My granny loved roses and had a whole bed of them alongside her cottage – are there any out there in your garden?"

"Absolutely," Agatha said as she rose and locked onto the girl's elbow to guide her to the door. "We'll make them our first stop. Look out there, dear. See those tall purple-flowered bushes? Those are Buddleia – also called Butterfly Bush. They mark the path to the rose beds. We'll head down that way and you can tell me what variety of roses your grandmother grew."

"Well," Meaghan said, a little uncertainly, "I recall there were pink ones and white ones..." she trailed off.

Oh brother, Agatha thought, mentally rolling her eyes, but she said: "I'll explain once we're standing in front of the bed with my floribundas."

"Um, okay," the girl said in a dubious tone. "But meanwhile, let me tell you about my granny's strawberries. They were the best, and she'd let me help her pick them, though, of course I ate almost as many as I picked! She'd tell me to stop or there'd be none left to make jam, and she made delicious jam! Which reminds me of that time..."

Getting her second wind, I see – I'll have to remedy that, Agatha decided and said: "Delighted to hear more. Let me adjust my hearing aid for outdoors."

Agatha reached up to the ear that just happened to be on the same side she had placed Meaghan and lowered the volume control. Firmly linking the girl's arm with her own, she pushed open the screen door and guided her captive to the serpentine path that wound through the gardens.

SILENCE AND COOL BREEZES

GENE RACKOVITCH

The old man drove into a rest area in Florida, tired after five hours on the road. At age seventy-two, long spells of driving weren't easy any more. He remembered how ten years ago he could drive all day and night to get to Florida from New York. Things change, old age was finally catching up to him. He went into the men's room, relieved himself, went back to his car and brought out a cooler.

He hunted out a picnic area at the rear of the main building, away from the throngs of tourists milling about it, and headed for where a few concrete over-hangs with matching benches were empty. One would afford him some solitude.

The welcome center's congestion of snowbirds and multi-offspring families heading for Orlando's Disney World made the old man a little anxious. Besides, it was lunchtime. He extracted a sandwich and a quart of milk from the cooler.

Flashbacks plagued him of late. He drifted from the rest stop to the Marine base in San Diego, returning from overseas duty after twenty-four months. The year, 1947. Remembering the mess hall in the boot camp where they were to be mustered out, the first meal back in the states. *Milk, ya couldn't keep enough of it on the tables*, he recalled. Fresh milk, deprived of it so long... *Americans,* he thought, *milk; that's us.* Powdered milk just didn't make it, it wasn't the same. He watched it disappear from the mess hall tables. Home at last, and milk.

All these years, all the changes, he drifted back to the rest stop. *My God, look at them, what a wonderful country we have!*

He surveyed the tourists. A breeze came up, he savored it, thinking. *My children, did I tell them about the cool breeze, that cleansing breeze so many years ago? How a breeze clears the air and creates the silence. My youngest, I remember, I introduced it to her in Pennsylvania at a motel off the road. Sunday morning, it was. I called her out of the room early that day. Remember.*

"Come here Jude, I want you to hear something."

"What is it dad?"

She came out brushing her hair.

"Sit a moment," he said

"What is it you want me to hear?"

"Listen... Listen," he pressed her.

"I don't hear anything."

"Yeah, Jude that's right...that's it, listen to the silence and feel the cool breeze, it cleanses everything from the air."

She sat quietly for a moment, then smiled.

"Hold it, it's precious," he told her.

She put her hand in his and they sat quietly.

Look at 'em, look at 'em...ya think they have any idea how all this came about? he wondered as he went back to surveying the mass of humanity at the rest stop.

He felt a breeze, it cooled him, and his mind went even further back. To a time some fifty-odd years ago as a replacement on a Higgins boat going into the beach at Iwo Jima; seeing a stack of wood piled there and wondering what they needed it for.

It was raining and foggy on the beach. Part of the fog was made by artillery fire being laid down by the Marines there. As he advanced up the beach with the other replacements, the stacked wood became more distinct. He stopped a passing Marine and asked what they needed the wood for.

"That ain't wood, boy, that's bodies."

"Oh, ya mean Jap bodies?"

"No boy, that's marines."

He looked at his comrades, saw the look in their eyes and wondered if his eyes showed the same fear he saw there; it said God help us. They moved forward.

They came to the island late in the campaign. Most of the resistance had been eliminated. Still, pockets of opposition prevailed. After ten days of constant engagement with the enemy, there was a pause in the action. Alone, while moving to a new position, he found himself under a high ridge that shielded him from any contact with the enemy.

He sat, removed his helmet, set his rifle aside; he then realized the air was clear. A soft breeze off the ocean blew away the tart odor of cordite that settled after a lull in fighting. A feeling of being home in Pennsylvania came over him, sitting on the shoulder of the road on the farm, corn fields extended on both sides, cherry trees bordered the fields full enough to canopy the road, the breeze just strong enough to scatter the fruit to the ground. He sat under one of the trees and gathered the fruit.

It was the first time he remembered that great feeling of quiet as it settled off a cool breeze. That's what he felt that day on Iwo Jima. He was about to get up and take his rifle and helmet when melancholia settled on him. He began to sob uncontrollably. The more he wanted to stop, the more his body was racked by it.

A gunnery sergeant surveying the area while leading a work party hauling satchel charges, saw the young Marine from a distance. He knew the boy. As his work party was waiting for instructions on how to proceed, he pointed the way, making sure they did not come in contact with the sobbing marine. He waited until they had moved on before he approached the overhang where the marine was.

Christ, not another one, the gunny thought. *I coulda swore that kid wouldn't break.* He knew what happened to men who couldn't take combat's uncertainty any more, how it could happen to anyone, even the best men. It didn't matter who you were.

There was no anger in him for those that quit the fighting, most were absorbed into other units; some ended in supply; others were completely out of it, ending up on a hospital ship and then home. He couldn't remember anyone that had to do the fighting condemning those who quit.

He recalled Stone during the battle of Saipan; he'd bolted, left the company for the rear. Realizing what he'd done, he begged the company commander to let him come back. The commander said no. The gunny sergeant spoke to the commander on the man's behalf. The commander relented and the man was reinstated. Two days later Stone was dead, killed by a sniper's bullet.

Yeah, he knew he was gonna get it. That's why he took off. Came back any way. Jesus, good men we got here.

Others passed through his mind. The uncertainty of it all could get to you; it disturbed him. *One minute everything's fine, the next ya get yer brains knocked out.*

There were those he knew that had the gift and never got a scratch. He looked to the sky and thought. *Ya can feel it comin' in, the shells, it does something to the air. Ya know it before ya hear it, before it goes off, some sorta pressure, ya can't explain it; it becomes instinctive to move. Ya jump into one hole, those with you jump in another, bingo they're gone! You're in the right one, they're not. Next thing ya know, there's a guy's arm layin' next to ya. It's Jo Jo's, ya know, 'cause ya see his tattoos on it. Jesus, he's gone and you're safe. Some say it's God on your side; I say its dumb ass luck.*

He's good, he thought as he watched the boy, *that kid is a good marine. He did everything asked of him, did some running, carrying messages between headquarters and the other platoons, didn't flinch when asked to put down fire when it was needed. He did the job. What happens to them?* He approached the marine.

Our marine came to realize why he had tears streaming down his cheeks. The wood came back to him. His mind went back to the beach and all the others he'd seen killed in just days of doing his job as a marine infantryman.

Oh Jesus, oh Jesus, they ain't gonna feel it, never gonna feel the soft breezes, never gonna have the pleasure again of feeling that soft breeze and the quiet that comes with it. Oh Christ, never gonna know again the great feeling of pleasure that you enjoy on this earth; the bliss of it all, never again, never again.

He calmed himself, brought his sleeve across his face and wiped the tears away.

"Hey, kid, ya okay?" The gunny asked as he arrived.

The young marine wanted to tell the sergeant how he felt, but thought better of it and decided not to.

"Come on, kid, we're takin' this stuff." He pointed to the satchel charge over his shoulder. "We're gonna close up some of them caves up on the hill. Gonna give 'em a chance to come out, if they don't, fuck 'em, then they're gonna stay fer ever."

"I'm comin' Sarg. I'm okay."

He picked up his rifle put on his helmet, and followed the gunnery sergeant.

I wonder if these tourists know what it cost for me and them to have this beautiful place on this marvelous day. Christ, I remember, I remember. At least I told one of my kids about the silence and cool breezes. I gotta somehow tell the rest of 'em.

He mulled it over and realized how much time had passed. He wiped a tear from his face with his sleeve.

They are really enjoying it all, that's good, that's good, he thought. He covered his cooler and set off for his car. "Nice place, nice place. Thanks," he said, while looking to the heavens, and he walked off.

I'D LIKE YOU TO KNOW

SUSAN ROSENSTREICH

For many years, or so it seemed then, I lived with my grandparents in their dark apartment that smelled of lemons and was lighted on Friday nights only by candles. Then my mother came to reclaim me. For the first few days, perhaps more, I refused most food, and cried as I wandered, lost, through the seven rooms of my family's first floor apartment. Like my grandparents', our apartment was dark, not only inside, but outside, too, encased in brick of a color that swallowed sunlight and breathed black coal dust onto the grey Chicago snow. Anchored in stony solitude, each house in our neighborhood was a continent away from all others, and though my grandparents lived only three streets from us, to return to them was to cross the steppes of my grandmother's homeland. But I was certain I would know the way. Not the whole way, just the part I needed to know until I got to the part that came next.

I knew about suitcases, and found one. In it I packed all my mother's shoes, then clasped the handle of the luggage with both hands and dragged it, thudding as it bumped, down the three steps of our foyer. I could see the street through the glass rectangles of the door, beveled so that the street appeared to be an ocean twisted into watery ribbons. Just beyond, I recognized the sidewalk leading to my grandparents' house. Still dragging the suitcase with both hands, I heard it bump down the curb and into the street. I was not halfway across when my mother came up behind me and, taking my hand, gently, as I think on it now, urged me back to our foyer. Then I took a nap. My grandmother was by my side when I woke up.

Some years later, we came to visit my grandparents and Chicago from our home far away. My mother had already taken me screaming to my first day of nursery school, my father had returned from the war, I had a tricycle of my own. But I would often dream of my grandparents. In one dream, my grandmother touched my shoulder and said my name. I had found my parents in our dining room, reading, and told them my grandmother was calling me. My mother heated water and gave it to me mixed with milk. I sat by our gas heater, warming myself inside and out as I drank her potion. Soon after that, we left early one morning to take a train to Chicago.

My grandmother was much changed. Her back was hunched. She wept and drew me into her lemony embrace. My mother and her parents spoke in their language. "The child has changed," said my grandmother. "Of course, Mama. She's four now." I refused to leave my grandparents' apartment when my mother rose to take me to her sister's house, two blocks away. My grandfather insisted I leave with my mother, but I gripped either my grandmother or her couch as my mother grasped my hand to lead me away. I could not be moved. My grandmother made me a bed on the couch. I could hear my grandfather in the kitchen where he was having tea. "I don't want the child here," he insisted in his language. And my grandmother answered in her language, "she is staying with me one night." And then silence with the smell of lemons.

The next morning, my mother came to take me away. I acquiesced. It had been a good night. My grandmother had slept beside me on the couch, and there had been no dreams, just my grandmother beside me. My mother was helping me into my coat, first one arm, then the other, then tying the ribbons of the coat's matching hat under my chin. My grandmother was weeping quietly and, in her language, she was telling my mother about a sister, someone I didn't know, my mother didn't know. Because she was dead. And she died, my grandmother was saying, after she was shot, because she ran after a train that was taking someone, perhaps her brother, I couldn't tell, or else she ran away from a train that was taking someone, perhaps her mother, I couldn't tell, and they shot her, my grandmother was saying in her language, first one arm, then the other, then one leg, then the other, then .... My mother covered my ears. "Hush. She shouldn't hear," my mother said in her mother's language. But I had heard. I knew. Now you know, too.

OUR GROUP

**THE NORTH FORK WRITERS GROUP
WAS FORMED IN 2010.
ITS MEMBERSHIP GENTLY EVOLVED TO
THIS CORE FELLOWSHIP - OUR BOOK'S**

Seven Voices

GENE RACKOVITCH
Greenport, NY

Gene was a Marine and entrepreneur. He founded the North Fork Writers Group to foster creativity in writing, which eventuality led to the *Seven Voices* represented in this anthology. He has published five books, with all being products of his life experiences. Gene's stories are told in a distinctive narrative style, as though he's sitting and talking one on one with a friend.

DAVID PORTEOUS
Mattituck, NY

Dave was a member of the Australian Writers' Guild for 30 years, but he has written all his life and had his poetry in several anthologies. Now a US citizen, he found new creative inspiration and camaraderie in the North Fork Writers Group. Dave is proud to be one of the **Seven Voices**, offering his wry tales of people trying to survive the impact of dysfunctional lives, their own and others' – his favorite theme.

KIT STORJOHANN
Greenport, NY

Kit is a photographer and meditation teacher who studied Creative Writing at Binghamton University. The focus of his writing has evolved to span various places and epochs throughout human history, illuminating the timeless interplay of the human spirit. Having found support and encouragement for his talents in the North Fork Writers Group, Kit is proud to contribute four of his stories to **Seven Voices**.

JOYCE deCORDOVA
Greenport, NY

Joyce and artist Hector deCordova lead creative lives. She is a mother of five and grandmother of seventeen. While being a businesswoman, guidance counselor and social worker have been her careers, her passion was always storytelling. Now, as a member of the North Fork Writers Group, Joyce can offer readers her imaginative mind and life insights and as one of our *Seven Voices*.

JEAN SCHWEIBISH
Mattituck, NY

Jean, a legal assistant and native Long Islander, earned a visual arts degree in photography at Empire State College. Still an ardent photographer, she has extended her creativity by honing a lifelong writing habit. As a member of the lively group whose work comprises this anthology, Jean feels honored to have her first published stories included in the diverse and original offerings found in **Seven Voices.**

SUSAN
ROSENSTREICH
Cutchogue, NY

Susan has kept a journal since the age of 8, recording her life in four countries and 17 schools before she earned her Doctorate in French at CUNY Graduate Center. Now, as Professor Emerita of Foreign Languages and Literatures at Dowling College, she escapes from her academic writing in North Fork Writers Group. Her stories are shaped by the different realities she has seen, laced with her life's worldly views.

TERESA TAYLOR
Greenport, NY

As a child, Teresa wrote narratives she modeled on her Brooklyn friends. As an adult, she has taught writing in high schools and to adults. Her talents as a writer have been acclaimed because of her published novel, *Family Matters*, which draws from her own life as fact-based fiction. Some of Teresa's tales in **Seven Voices** remind her of those she invented as a girl, but now colored by her extensive life experiences.

The New
Atlantian Library

NewAtlantianLibrary.com
or AbsolutelyAmazingeBooks.com
or AA-eBooks.com